COME ON, FOLKS, LET'S HEAR IT FOR THE NEWCOMERS TO THE NEIGHBORHOOD

Listen to your President and your First Lady.

Don't be prejudiced against the Martians just because they have those ugly space suits, monstrous heads, nasty faces, and other disgusting features that make them the last beings in the universe that you'd like to take out for lunch.

Instead, remember that they're our neighbors in space. Roll out the welcome wagon for their three thousand flying saucers. Extend the hand of hospitality. Show them what Earthlings are really made of.

Of course, they have their own ways of finding that out. They can check out the pieces after they blast us to bits. . . .

MARS ATTACKS!

They come in peace.

Not.

OTHER BOOKS BY JONATHAN GEMS

PLAYS

The Tax Exile
Three Plays

A Novel by
Jonathan Gems
Based on his screen story and screenplay
Based upon Mars Attacks,
a property of the Topps Company

Ⓢ

A SIGNET BOOK

SIGNET
Published by the Penguin Group
Penguin Books USA Inc., 375 Hudson Street,
New York, New York 10014, U.S.A.
Penguin Books Ltd, 27 Wrights Lane,
London W8 5TZ, England
Penguin Books Australia Ltd,
Ringwood, Victoria, Australia
Penguin Books Canada Ltd, 10 Alcorn Avenue,
Toronto, Ontario, Canada M4V 3B2
Penguin Books (N.Z.) Ltd., 182-190 Wairau Road,
Auckland 10, New Zealand

Penguin Books Ltd, Registered Offices:
Harmondsworth, Middlesex, England

First published by Signet, an imprint of Dutton Signet,
a division of Penguin Books USA Inc.

First Printing, December, 1996
10   9   8   7   6   5   4   3   2   1

 REGISTERED TRADEMARK—MARCA REGISTRADA

Printed in the United States of America

For Tim Burton
who co-wrote the screenplay
and didn't ask for a credit.

Chapter 1

Oh! thus be it ever, when freemen shall stand
Between their loved homes and the war's desolation!
Blest with victory and peace, may the heaven-rescued land
Praise the Power that hath made and preserved us a
nation.
Then conquer we must, for our cause it is just,
And this be our motto: "In God is our trust."
And the star-spangled banner in triumph shall wave
O'er the land of the free and the home of the brave.

> —Francis Scott Key (1799–1843)
> Designated the American national
> anthem by Congress in 1931.

"Look at these shoes," said Sylvia. "Twenty-eight dollars."

Alfred Lee looked at the high-heeled, shiny white pumps with the crisscross straps that gripped his wife's feet.

"Very pretty."

They were in the kitchen. Alfred returned to bagging the garbage. Sylvia knew he would not criticize her for buying these frivolous shoes. These shoes would nourish her through the summer.

Alfred and Sylvia were immigrants from the Philippines. They had met thirteen years before at an English class in Los Angeles. The first time he laid eyes on her, Alfred Lee was smitten with the spirited Sylvia, who worked as an assistant cutter for a small clothes company called Playdeck Fashions.

But Sylvia didn't take him seriously and called him "Halibut Man" because he smelled of fish.

In those early immigrant days Alfred worked long hours at a fish cannery and saved all his money. His ancestors had all been fishermen but Alfred hated fish, hated the sea, hated the Philippines, and wanted to escape. He knew before he could walk, while he was still crawling, that he had to get away—as far away as possible.

When he was twelve he told his family of his precious dream. They called it a flight of fancy and took no notice. But he never let go of his precious dream, so unusual for a poor Catholic Filipino. One day—one bright day in the far distant future—he would do it. He was determined to do it or die in the attempt. One day, come hell or high water, he would become an American Midwestern cattle farmer.

Back in those L.A. salad days, Sylvia loved to go out with her girlfriends and "get in trouble." They would go to the community dances, the parties in Manhattan Beach, the bars around the marina and they would dance and flirt and drink kamikazes. Sometimes, on a Saturday night, they would borrow her brother's low-rider Ford Galaxie and drive all the way to Hollywood, so they could cruise down Hollywood Boulevard and yell wild things to the beautiful cholo gang boys with their gleaming biceps and tattoos, coolly parading in their drug-money-bought muscle cars. It was fun.

So, why did she marry Halibut Man? She sometimes wondered that herself. Maybe it was because he loved her? But she could not respect a man who loved her because she had little love for herself. Maybe it was because his will was stronger than hers? Or maybe it was because he had a precious dream—something to follow, something that gave a purpose and shape to life?

Anyway, she rarely regretted having married him—even when she felt lonesome for the excitement of city life. And now, twelve and a half years later, they had two children—a ten-year-old son named Junior and an eight-year-old daughter, Bing (named after her grandmother). And they lived very happily on a 400-acre cattle ranch in Kentucky, eight miles north of Lockjaw.

"I'm going to start dinner."

"Okay."

Alfred opened the back door and picked up the two bulging plastic bags of garbage.

Sylvia glanced out the window at the low distant hills glowing in the sunset. This was her favorite time of day. This was when she liked to organize dinner and listen to the birds competing in their twilight-time songfest. She had learned to distinguish between the sharp high cries of the grasshopper sparrows, the mournful notes of the cowbirds, and the arpeggios of the Kentucky warblers. Tonight, though, the birds were oddly silent.

The screen door slammed as Alfred went out the back door. Tomorrow was trash-collecting day. As he headed for the trash cans, he noticed a strange burnt smell in the air, then he heard the sound of a tractor. Dwight McCutcheon was coming down the road on his old Massey-Ferguson.

Alfred liked Dwight, a farmhand on the neighboring ranch. Dwight was a real hillbilly, about sixty years old, with leathery skin and small bright blue eyes like a chaffinch.

They said Dwight was lazy, but he wasn't; he was just slow. The bartender at the Tainted Lady Lounge in Lockjaw told Alfred that Dwight's parents were "closely related." Maybe that was

so, but Dwight had the most sprightly tempera-
ment of any man Alfred had ever known. He
was always cheerful.

"Howdy, Mister Lee. What is this? Filipino
New Year's?"

"No, why you say that?"

Dwight stopped his tractor out front by the
trash cans.

" 'Cause you're cooking up a feast. You can
smell it all the way from the interstate. What is
it, a barbecue?"

Alfred could smell it, too, the rich smell of
grilling hamburger—*lots* of grilling hamburger.
Alfred looked around, mystified.

"But it's not coming from here."

They both heard it at the same time, and they
instantly knew what it was. It's the one thing a
rancher dreads—a stampede.

If you have experienced an earthquake, you
never forget it, so, too, a cattle stampede. But
stampedes happened on a trail drive, usually at
night, usually during a storm, when the live-
stock were nervous, when a clap of thunder
could set them off.

A stampede was often started by one jumpy
animal. Alfred would try to identify the jumpy
steers before the beginning of a drive and tie
their hind legs. Dwight used an old cowboy's
trick. He would single out the potential offend-

ers and sew up their eyelids. It took about a week for the thread to rot, allowing the eyes to open, by which time they were "broke in."

In a stampede, the herd quickly became a monstrous, irresistible force, destroying everything in its path. Dwight would never forget, on a cattle drive to Wichita, finding a man mashed into the ground as flat as a pancake.

"What's that noise?" said Dwight.

Both Alfred and Dwight knew exactly what that noise was but they were in denial. **Denial**. Denial/di'ni(e)l/n (1528) **1:** refusal to satisfy a request or desire; **2a** (1): refusal to admit the truth or reality (as of a statement or charge); (2): assertion that an allegation is false; **b:** refusal to acknowledge a person or a thing; **3:** negation in logic; **4:** a large river in Africa.

Why, when we can't deal with something, do we react like an ostrich who has a brain the size of peanut? Humans are the most complex and evolved of all animals, yet fear, in one instant, will undo a million years of evolution.

"Yes, what is that noise?" said Alfred. The primeval force of denial had them clamped.

The front door of the house flew open and Sylvia, Junior, Bing, and the dog, Marvin, ran out. They were yelling something. But Alfred couldn't hear because the air was resounding

with four thousand galloping hooves and a ca-
cophony of anguished bovine moans.

Around the bend in the road came a thousand
head of cattle, and they were all on fire!

"Oh, my Lord!" exclaimed Dwight.

Things happened very quickly after that. The
burning cows stampeded toward them. Alfred,
Sylvia, and the kids clambered up on the tractor.
The blazing cattle crashed by on both sides. For
a brief second Junior saw Marvin trying to leap
up to join them, but he was knocked aside and
lost under the pounding hooves. Junior didn't
hear the dog scream. He didn't see the dog get
crushed to a pulp—there was too much noise,
too much flame, too much thick black smoke.

Dwight, Alfred, Sylvia, and the kids clung to
one another, too terrified to speak. The crowded
tractor was like an island in a sea of flaming
beef.

Clinging to her father on the jolting tractor,
Bing noticed a different sound behind the drum-
ming of the hooves. The sound was strange, oth-
erworldly and throbbing. It seemed to be
coming from behind the house. The howling
cows thundered past. She could barely see
through the smoke, but she saw something—
something very surprising. It was oval-shaped
and silver and it was hovering in the sky behind
the house.

"Look! What's that?" She pointed.

Alfred followed her gaze, and knew what it was. He had seen pictures of flying saucers on the covers of magazines and he had once met a member of the Aetherius Society who had explained that aliens visited the Earth in flying saucers in the 1930s in order to introduce human beings to the benefits of megadoses of vitamins.

The burning herd was past them now, stampeding away down the road and across the field.

"Look at that!" said Sylvia.

They were now all staring at the flying saucer. Junior's eyes were bugging out. He couldn't wait to tell his friends from school. Alfred was thinking that maybe the saucer had something to do with what happened to his cattle, and would it be covered by insurance? Dwight could see the spaceship but his brain couldn't comprehend it, so it converted the visual information into the shape of a small white cloud, and he wondered: What's that weird little cloud doing there?

All at once the flying saucer shot straight up, traveling so fast that, a moment later, it was a silver dot in the twilight sky. Alfred blinked and it was gone.

Chapter 2

"The planet Earth is a speck of dust, remote and alone in the void. There are powers in the universe inscrutable and profound."

—Leslie Stevens in *The Outer Limits: The Official Companion* by David J. Schow and Jeffrey Frentzen

The Solar System consists of the Sun, an average-size star, surrounded by nine planets and their moons, together with a bunch of smaller asteroids. The Universe is so incredibly vast that it must contain untold numbers of other solar systems, but our own is the only one we know anything about.

The planet closest to the sun is Mercury. Its surface temperature is hot enough to melt iron. Next comes Venus, a planet covered in dense clouds of acid vapor. It is almost as hot as Mercury because its thick atmosphere of carbon dioxide traps heat like a greenhouse.

Some scientists believe that a human-friendly atmosphere could be created on Venus by introducing blue-green algae. Blue-green algae are primitive plant cells that absorb carbon dioxide and excrete oxygen, and can survive great temperatures.

Donald Kessler, the well-known British scientist, has calculated it would take 160 years to oxygenate Venus sufficiently for humans to breathe there.

The remaining inner planets are Earth, the only planet on which life has developed, and red, dusty Mars. Outside of these planets lies a belt of rocky lumps known as the asteroids. These are millions of dead, useless swirling rocks. Then comes Jupiter, the biggest planet, famous for its red spot. Then comes Saturn, with its famous rings. Saturn, the second largest planet in the Solar System, is weird because it floats in a bubble of water.

The outermost planets are the well-known Uranus, Neptune, and baby Pluto, which is no bigger than our own neighbor moon.

When they portray space in the movies they usually show it like nighttime on earth: blackness peppered with stars. This is totally wrong. Space is so bright you need heavy-duty sunglasses because there are no layers of atmosphere to filter the sunlight. It is also hot because, again, there are no layers of atmosphere to shield you from the sun.

But the light and heat of space didn't bother the little flying saucer, which sped happily away from Earth, traveling at just below the speed of light. Any faster and it would have a) become invisible, and b) started going backward in time, according to accepted views of physics that may, of course, be wrong.

The flying saucer, which was a dull silver in color and about the size of an average four-bedroom house, was shaped like a mix between the nose cone of a turbofan engine and a Chinese coolie's hat. It looked like the renditions of flying saucers seen in '50s science fiction films such as *Invasion of the Flying Saucers* or *Plan 9 From Outer Space.*

This is not surprising because the designs of the spacecraft in those films were actually based upon real UFO sightings. Yuri Gagarin, the first man in space, described seeing exactly such a craft when he orbited the Earth in Vostok 1.

At 18,400 miles from the surface of the Earth, the spaceship changed direction, tripled its speed, and vanished from human sight—were there human eyes to see it, which there weren't.

But there *were* alien eyes. A host of alien eyes had been tracking the saucer for the entirety of its mission; and behind these alien eyes were brains—large brains.

Mars is a smaller planet than Earth but the Martian day is very similar, being 24 hours 37 minutes at an obliquity of 23 27' compared to 23 29' for the Earth. Because of its greater distance from the Sun and its thinner atmosphere, the surface temperature is much lower, scarcely rising to freezing point on warm summer afternoons.

The poles of Mars are covered with ice caps that expand and contract with the seasons just as do the Earth's. But there is little water vapor in the Martian air and, because there are no living organisms on the surface, there is little oxygen.

The surface of Mars has been photographed in great detail by the Space Probes Mariner 9 and the Viking orbiters. The photographs have revealed a surprising variety of scenery. Vast areas of Mars are desert plains strewn with ruddy rocks and soil. These are old lava flows that give the planet its red hue. Other regions, mostly in the South, show the scars of bombardment by huge meteoric bodies that collided with the planet in the remote past.

Giant volcanoes rise from the plains. Fractures and faults—sometimes called "canals"— are easily seen. The largest of these is the enormous canyon known as Coprates. This is 2,485 miles long and two miles deep.

No surface water exists on Mars but, in the past, water must have flowed because there is ample evidence that water, or a similar fluid, eroded extensive portions of the surface.

At less than a million miles from the Red Planet, the flying saucer decelerated, came out of hyperdrive, and shot out a flare. The flare bloomed like a spreading white bloodstain against the spangly velvet backdrop of the universe.

On the surface of Mars, eighteen miles north of the Coprates canyon, the signal was observed by a periscope. This shiny machine-tooled object protruded incongruously from a small crater. The periscope retracted, and, moments later, a deep humming sound began. The vast, cratered plain began to vibrate. Something noisy was happening underground.

Next to where the periscope had been, was a larger crater—almost four hundred feet across. If you looked into it you would see, about thirty feet down, a metallic surface as flat as a skating rink. This was both roof and door to what lay below.

This roof/door slid open—disappearing into the crater's rocky walls—and a large Martian warship rose majestically, out of the shadows.

This saucer-shaped object rotated at such a high speed that it created its own antigravity field.

Farther off, another crater opened and a second spaceship emerged. Then, all over the vast plain, spaceships rose out of craters—craters that had been adapted for use as ship-bays and silos.

The noise was deafening and the ground shook as the massive Martian fleet ascended through the thin atmosphere, and rose into the pale red sky like three thousand spinning Frisbees.

Beyond the planet's atmosphere, the armada assembled into arrow-shaped formations. At the apex of the first arrow was the Martian leader's flagship.

When Phobos and Deimos, the twin moons of Mars, were safely behind them, the flagship altered course. The other 2,999 ships smoothly followed suit. On this new course, traveling at nine factors above light, they would reach Earth's orbit in less than forty-six hours.

Chapter **3**

The trip to Washington had been everything that they both had dreamed of and hoped for and more . . . to them it seemed as beautiful as a vision of white-pillared Paradise.

—Frances Parkinson Keyes

As might be expected, Washington, D.C., the capital city of America, boasts a cornucopia of architectural delights. Included here are all the grand styles inherited from Europe, as well as buildings that reflect an Eastern flavor—*viz.*: the Islamic Mosque—and a profusion of home-grown and hybrid forms, such as the Tail O' The Pup hamburger restaurant and the Arco gas station on 23rd Street.

In the history of Washington's architecture are two distinct strands: the domestic and the public, which are sometimes separate and sometimes intertwined.

The oldest house in the District of Columbia is Old Stone House in Georgetown. This was built in 1766 and is a good example of the solid unpretentious building of the Colonial period.

The period immediately after the American Revolution is known as the Federal period and was greatly influenced by the modified Georgian style created in Scotland by the Adam brothers. Official buildings of the Federal period include the graceful residence designed by James Hoban as the President's mansion and known today as the White House.

That day, in the Oval Office, five very important men were having a very important meeting. Historians would later note the time as 11:25 in the morning on Tuesday, May 10, in the Year of Our Lord 2003.

The men gathered on that fateful day were as follows: the celebrated British scientist Professor Donald Kessler, the White House press secretary, Jerry Ross, the legendary, bullet-headed General Jack Decker, the popular African-American General Bill Casey, and Mr. James Dale, the President of the United States.

President Dale was examining a sheaf of fuzzy black-and-white photographs of the Martian fleet. He couldn't quite believe this was happening.

"What's your take on this, Jerry?" he said, turning to his friend, the press secretary.

"The people are gonna love it!"

Jerry Ross knew a good media story when he saw one.

"Our only decision is whether to ambush the six o'clock news or hold out for prime time."

By nature, President Dale thought very quickly—but this got him in trouble, so he tried to think slowly.

"Hmm . . ."

"Screw the press," barked General Decker. "This situation is on a need-to-know. We gotta keep this top secret and go immediately to Defcon Four."

General Jack Decker was seventy-two years old and fitter than most men half his age. He worked out three hours a day—an hour of running, an hour of lifting weights, and an hour of yoga. Not only was he a four-star general, he was also a real soldier. He'd seen action in Korea and Vietnam, and received a Purple Heart for killing seven Vietcong in one night with a bowie knife. Jerry Ross thought he was a big fag.

"Please, Mr. President," Jerry pleaded. "We *can't sit on this!*"

But the President turned to General Bill Casey. "General, what's your opinion?"

General Casey was reclining on the antique Teddy Roosevelt Chesterfield, radiating warmth and reassurance. Born in the ghetto, in East St. Louis, Missouri, he was raised by his grandmother, mother, and four sisters, who had all loved him very much. Today he was an African-American success story.

"Well, sir, how do we know they're hostile?"

Decker almost exploded.

"They've got thousands of warships circling the planet!"

Casey put the tips of his fingers together, pursed his lips and raised an eyebrow. "Do we *know* they're warships?"

President Dale enjoyed the rivalry between these two warhorses, but he didn't have time for it now.

"Professor, what do we know about them?"

Professor Donald Kessler was standing by the window, sucking on his unlit pipe. He wore a tweed suit and horn-rimmed glasses. Born in Liverpool, England, the only son of a widowed mother, he discovered, at an early age, an aptitude for schoolwork. Devoting himself zealously to his studies, he rose rapidly through the ranks of academia, attaining the position of professor of astronautics at Oxford University at the unusually young age of thirty-three. He had the tremendous self-confidence of a man who had never scored less than 90 percent in any exam.

"We know they're extremely advanced technologically, which suggests, very strongly, that they're peaceful. An advanced civilization is, by definition, not barbaric. This is a great day, Mr. President," said Donald Kessler, sucking on his pipe, "I'm extremely excited."

General Decker scowled. Who was this English ninny?

"Good!" The President clapped his hands and rubbed them together. "Extraterrestrial life! You're right Jerry, the people are gonna love it. This is a momentous occasion . . ."

General Decker glared at the President and thought: this man is the Commander-In-Chief— can you believe it? The guy is a total flub. God help us if we get in any trouble.

President Dale's eyes were shining. "It's a day we've all dreamed of since . . . since the caveman first stared up into the night sky and wondered 'Am I Alone?' "

Jerry Ross, General Casey, and Donald Kessler nodded. They liked the President when he was possessed by the gab. At these moments you could detect his Irish ancestry. He turned to Jerry Ross.

"What do you say we go all-media? . . . and

I'll wear my blue Cerruti suit. And I'll need a good speech. Statesmanlike. Historical, but warm, neighborly. Abraham Lincoln meets Leave It To Beaver—you know the kind of thing. . . ."

"Yessir!" said Jerry.

At the other end of the White House, past the security station, if you take a left and go straight through the Grant Wing, past the Rose Room, up the big staircase—where you can get a good view of the Nancy Reagan chandelier—and, at the top, hang a dogleg past the portrait of Dwight D. Eisenhower, you will be at the marbled entrance to the Roosevelt Room.

The Roosevelt Room was where Marsha Dale, the First Lady, was currently waging her war to redecorate the White House. She and her fifteen-year-old-daughter, Taffy (who had been granted the day off school because of "tummy trouble") were looking at swatches of material laid out on the Louis XVI sofa by the renowned decorator Regis de la Mole.

"I think . . . too old-fashioned," said Marsha, and discarded the organza.

She picked up a cotton print.

"Oh, Nancy had this in the library, didn't she?"

"I thought perhaps the watered silk?" said Regis, gently lifting the Chinese silk so that it glittered translucently in the light from the bay windows.

"And this week it's on sale."

The First Lady wrinkled her nose, in that characteristic gesture that so entranced the young James Dale when they took their first strolls together below the ivy walls of Old Yale.

"I hardly think I need worry about it being on sale. My husband *is* the leader of the Free World."

She turned to her daughter, a dark, pretty young girl whose moods were varying states of melancholy.

"What do you think, Taffy?"

Taffy didn't really hate her mother. How could you hate someone who wasn't even a person? But she resented playing a part so her mother could pretend they had a relationship. Taffy was waiting. Her whole life was waiting. She was waiting to grow up so she could be free, do real things, and have real relationships with real people.

"Why don't you leave the Roosevelt Room the way the Roosevelts wanted it?"

"Because Eleanor Roosevelt was too fond of chintz, that's why!"

Taffy was suddenly hit by a wave of exasperation. "Mother, this is *not your house!*"

"Taffy, if you're going to be a pest, I'm just

going to have to ignore you!" She turned her back on Taffy and examined the silk.

Regis had taken out his camera. He had an idea to change the mood. Everyone likes getting their picture taken, right?

"Excuse me, First Lady, could I take a photograph? You look so lovely in this morning light."

Marsha Dale glanced at him suspiciously.

"It's just for my scrapbook."

"Oh, all right," she said, her sense of dignity restored. "But make it quick." Taffy watched, sullen and alone, as her mother struck one of her First Lady poses and Regis focused his single-lens reflex camera and snapped.

Chapter 4

"No man is a hypocrite in his pleasures."

—Samuel Johnson

Las Vegas, Nevada, is a city devoted entirely to entertainment. It is the fastest growing city in the United States, which proves it must be the kind of city people want. At the beginning of the twenty-first century, entertainment is what people crave. Let's face it—what else is there? Finally, after four thousand years of civilization, the world was waking up to the fact that hedonic values rule.

What exactly are hedonic values? Simply, a set of principles based upon the concept that pleasure is cool.

Primatologists coined the terms "hedonic" and "anhedonic" in order to classify two types of ape. Basically, the hedonic monkey doesn't fight and the anhedonic monkey does fight.

A typical example of the anhedonic ape is the baboon. Baboons establish their place in the hierarchy through physical combat. The toughest baboon becomes king—and has all the females he wants. He will mercilessly murder the children of the previous baboon king so that his progeny (and genetic material) will dominate. In Baboon-World might is right and only the strong survive.

The price the baboon king pays for his dominance is he must defend the baboon troop from outside aggressors. When the leopard—who likes to eat baboon flesh—stalks the troop, the baboon king does battle. He will fight the leopard, distracting him from the troop, who can escape to safety. Usually the leopard will kill him. Baboons are nothing if not heroic. General Decker's ex-wife once called him a baboon, not realizing how zoologically accurate she was being.

The hedonic ape is a monkey who dances. A typical example of the hedonic ape is the chimpanzee. Chimps love to display themselves—to dance, to clown, to vocalize—in a word, to entertain. The most talented chimp entertainer is elected king of the troop, and is admired by the alpha females who willingly become his brides.

When the leopard stalks the chimpanzee troop, the chimp king gets his attention by displaying himself in many eccentric and fascinating ways. Some chimps can imitate the sounds of a female leopard in heat, or, if the aggressor is a female, the sounds of infant leopards mewling for milk. The chimp king's box of tricks will divert the leopard long enough for the troop to flee to safety. And, more often than not, the chimp king's antics will so alter the leopard's mood that the leopard will lose interest in lunch altogether.

Anthropologists, sociologists, and psychologists recognize both hedonic and anhedonic characteristics in human nature. A clear example is the rivalry between the U.S. and the Soviet Union back in the 1960s. The frantic missile buildup on both sides was typical anhedonic baboon behavior. While the Space Race, on the other hand, was pure hedonic chimp.

When the Soviets put poor Yuri Gagarin in space, the U.S. experienced a massive drop in self-esteem and status. But later, when the U.S. put Armstrong on the moon—oh boy! that was sweet! And the Soviet Union never recovered from this blow to its ego.

So, Las Vegas is a hedonic city, peopled by chimps who gain status through their ability to entertain. There are actors, singers, dancers, acrobats, comedians, conjurers—performers of every stripe. The artists and craftsmen who designed and built the famous neon signs, the architects and decorators who fashioned the dazzling hotels, everyone who made—and makes—Vegas what it is today—all the way down to the costumed cocktail waitresses—all are chimps.

Along the main Vegas strip you can boggle at the new Stratosphere—tallest tower in the U.S., with a roller-coaster ride on top of it. The Tropicana and the Stardust still seduce with their quaint sixties vibe of sin. The Treasure Island, a Steve Wynn Hotel, with its artificial lake where a sea battle between two galleons is staged every hour; Circus Circus (historically the first of these "theme" hotels), where acrobats perform all day above the slot machines; the Mirage, with its mechanical volcano that erupts every hour; Caesar's Palace, where they built a shopping mall in the style of Ancient Rome, and hourly make the statues come alive; the MGM Grand—biggest of all—with its 'Wizard Of Oz' motif; New York, New York—a distilled re-creation of Manhattan; the Excalibur—all medieval pageantry; the Luxor—a big dark dose of Ancient Egypt; the Ponderosa, owned by Arthur Land, where cowboy gunfights occur every half hour and the waitresses dress like saloon whores; the Rio—all samba and papaya and Brazilian beauties . . . and fifty more such wild establishments . . . the whole city is committed to fantasy, escape, and entertainment.

Gambling, the bread and butter of the town, is, of course, one of the earliest ways humanity found to escape and defy the realities of life. But perhaps it's not so much an escape from life as an escape to a better life—a life of continuous stimulation, continuous entertainment. Fifty years from now, all cities will be like Las Vegas. London and Paris are already turning into theme parks. . . .

The Luxor Hotel and Casino, as is well known, was built (apparently with some difficulty) in the form of a colossal black pyramid. There is an enormous golden sphinx in front of it, which stares mysteriously across the airport and the Nevada scrub beyond. It doesn't look out of place because everything looks out of place in Las Vegas.

It was 4:30 P.M. on Tuesday, May 10, and Byron Williams was halfway through his shift. Byron, a big black man of fifty-five, had once been famous. Thirty years before he'd been the heavyweight boxing champion of the world. But now he was a greeter at the Luxor and dressed in an ill-fitting pharoah costume.

How the mighty are fallen! Byron Williams had run through $18 million in nineteen years. His managers had stolen from him. His business partners had stolen from him. His friends had stolen from him. About the only person who hadn't ripped him off was his wife, Louise. But this didn't stop Byron from blaming her.

Louise, an ex-beauty queen from Steamboat, Colorado, took a lot of beatings, but one day she'd had enough. She took the kids, went to stay with her aunt in Washington, D.C., and filed for divorce.

Now, Byron lived alone in a condo across from the Luxor. He had been in a state of atonement for the past eight years. He'd quit drinking and gone to counseling for his rage. And now, the bull was finally tamed.

Byron smiled as the Mother Superior took his picture. He was at the edge of the casino, near the entrance to the 3-D Tutankhamen Ride, posing with three very excited Carmelite nuns.

"Thank you, thank you!" said the Mother Superior.

"I saw you fight Sonny Liston in sixty-nine!" said one of the nuns.

Byron chuckled. "Is that right? Were you a nun back then?"

"Oh, yes!" replied the Mother Superior. "We've always been fight fans, haven't we, sisters?"

"Oh, yes!" echoed the others.

The public address system crackled and a

voice boomed through the hall: "Byron Williams, telephone. Byron Williams."

"That's me. Would you excuse me, ladies?" Byron bowed politely to the nuns. They nodded and smiled. These women were all in their late fifties, but they had the liveliness of teenage girls. Why do nuns have so much vim? Maybe it's God?

"Thank you so much!" they cried. "Thank you! Thank you!"

Byron walked through the busy casino. At the slots, an elderly white-haired lady was playing three machines, clutching a small, white plastic bucket filled with nickels. Her name was Dolores Snyder and she'd had a couple of bourbons and she felt lucky.

The casino hummed and clattered and jingled. Although it was 4:30 in the afternoon, it felt like 10 o'clock at night. It always felt like that in the casino—like a *Twilight Zone* episode where the clock started at 10 and stopped at 11—going back to 10 again—and everyone was doomed to repeat what they were doing between 10 and 11 for all eternity.

Byron headed through an avenue of blackjack tables, toward the staff station where there was a house phone.

"Hey, Byron, how's it going?"

Byron turned his head. It was Arthur Land

and Barbara, his wife. What were they doing here?

"Good, Art, thanks." said Byron. "Hey, Barbara."

"Hi." Barbara smiled with her sad, panicky eyes.

Art took Barbara's arm, waved at Byron, and headed for the Anubis Lounge.

Art was a big honcho in Vegas. Born in Reno, Nevada, he'd made money with a bunch of bingo operations. He'd had twenty-four bingo halls all over the state before he sold out and bought 51 percent of the Ponderosa. He was soon to open a new hotel named "The Galaxy," which was currently under construction.

Byron had known Art and Barbara for years. Art had tried to lure him over to the Ponderosa, but Byron liked the Luxor. The Luxor fitted his state of mind. It was like a tomb. Sometimes he would look around the spookily lit interior of the pyramid, with its sarcophagi and Osiris statues, and think: I'm dead and buried.

Byron didn't like Art too much. The guy was a pushy, noisy, flashy, self-satisfied jerk. Besides, he had the worst taste in clothes. He dressed like a country singer from Branson, in gaudy tailored suits encrusted with rhinestones, Stetson hat, bolo tie, and cowboy boots. If Art had gone to charm school, he should have gotten a refund.

Barbara was different. She had the vulnerability of the recovering alcoholic—something he could relate to. Byron found her very attractive. Why did the worst guys always get the best chicks?

As Byron crossed to the staff station, he noticed Mr. Bava, one of the casino managers, watching him. He ignored him and picked up the blinking house phone. It was Louise, his ex-wife, calling from Washington.

"I'm sorry to call you at work, but I'm losing my mind. The boys haven't been back for two nights and I don't know where they are! The teacher says they weren't in school. What am I gonna do?"

"Listen, sweetie," said Byron "you're doing the best you can. They're at that age. But if I was around, this wouldn't happen."

Louise was sitting by the window in the small living room of her apartment in Washington, D.C. On the sideboard was a framed photograph of her two sons Cedric and Neville. Outside, in the far distance, could be seen the back of the Capitol building. Her apartment was cheap but respectable, and she kept it neat and clean.

"Let me come back. Let me come back, Louise. I've changed."

"I don't know, Byron. A leopard don't change its spots."

"This one has," he said, and he meant it.

Louise's face and body had thickened since she was voted the prettiest girl in Colorado, but she still had her looks. She was forty-six, but she looked thirty-six. Like most Americans she was a mutt—but what an exotic one! The blood that mingled in her veins was part African, part Spanish, and part Cherokee Indian.

"I wish I could believe it," said Louise.

Byron felt someone's eyes on him. He looked around. Mr. Bava was glaring at him. He wasn't supposed to take calls at work.

"Louise, the casino manager's giving me the evil eye. I'd better go. I'll call you later, okay? You still cool with me coming to Washington?"

"Yeah, sure, 'course I am. Take care, honey. 'Bye."

Louise put the phone down and sighed. She still loved Byron Williams. He was still the greatest thing that had ever happened to her. But could she trust him now? She knew, deep down, that people don't change. And Byron had always been one unpredictable, crazy son of a bitch.

In the Anubis Lounge, in a booth, Arthur Land was telling his wife, Barbara, about his day.

"So I said to her: 'What in hell do you think you're doing? You don't open the door that way! You call me on the intercom first!'"

"She's new. Take it easy. There's no need to get hysterical."

"Hey, there's a lot riding on this. I could lose my shirt. I'm *entitled* to get hysterical!" Art raised his glass of malt whiskey to his lips and slurped. Barbara winced.

"Do you have to drink in front of me?"

Art shot her a glance, under hooded eyes. "You're a friggin' adult. Just cope."

Barbara's whole body was tense. She wanted a drink. But she didn't want a drink. She hated alcohol. For the past twelve years she'd been in an alcoholic haze. Her life hadn't been her own. Now she was sober and proud of it. It had taken a lot of willpower and strength—and it still did. She'd had to develop new emotional and spiritual muscles. She had to work them out every day. "One day at a time" as they said in AA. She liked these new muscles—they had given her a new confidence that was spreading into other areas of her life. She stood up to Art now—and he didn't like it.

"It doesn't help me that all we ever do is sit around bars."

"Hey, it's work, baby, okay? I'm studying the lighting, the decor, the traffic flow."

Barbara knew a lot about Art's business operations—and they were nothing if not shady. In recent months, amazed by how much time she had now that she wasn't drinking, she'd taken up reading—books about moral philosophy and spiritual growth.

"If I'd known you were gonna turn into a crook, I never would have married you."

"I'm not a crook," said Art. "I'm ambitious. There's a difference."

Barbara looked at him doubtfully.

"And if you think you can make a nickel in this town without knowing how to dally round a few curves, well . . ." he chuckled, "you don't know diddley-squat about the gaming industry."

A voice screamed in Barbara's head. It was saying: "This society stinks! Nothing's going on but an obscene violent decay of the human spirit and the ecosystem!"

Art looked at her. He was pissed at her. If he wasn't going to get support from his wife, then screw her, she could get lost. He didn't need her. He'd dump her—divorce her—get someone younger. How old was she—thirty-five? Hell, he'd get a twenty-five-year-old and, who knows? maybe even have kids?

The trick would be to get rid of her without losing a big chunk of change. He'd have to hide some of his assets. Get his lawyer, Joe Weinberg, on it.

Joe could figure it out. But, for right now, his priority was the new hotel. He didn't need any headaches. He'd keep her sweet.

"The Galaxy is gonna be the best hotel in Vegas," said Art. "The best. I'm gonna make you proud of me. I promise."

"But, don't you realize what you're doing? You're destroying the Earth! All this greed—all this money system—we're destroying everything!"

"Okay, okay, baby, take it easy, keep your voice down. I got friends here."

Art's glass was empty. He looked around and noticed a very attractive waitress at the bar. This was Cindy Gomez, a beautiful woman. He caught her eye and lifted his glass.

"Sugar! Hit me one more time will ya?"

Barbara scowled at him. "Stop flirting with the waitress!"

Art smiled to himself, reached into his pocket and took out a handful of chips. He gave Barbara his "Labrador puppy" look and clinked the chips in his hands.

"Go on over to roulette. Play our anniversary. And stay offa black."

He handed her the chips. She looked at him and melted. He knew how she loved to gamble. He could be sweet sometimes, even if he was a crook.

"All right, honey."

She got up, leaned over and kissed him lightly on the lips.

"See you later."

"Okay, sweetheart," said Art.

He watched her go, then turned his attention to the pretty waitress. She was beautiful. She was so beautiful his teeth hurt.

Chapter 5

"Anything for a quiet life."

—Thomas Middleton

Manhattan is a machine, fueled by the millions of people who pour through its streets and subways each day, many of them locked into an exhausting but addictive lifestyle that makes anywhere else seem slow and dull. These days, the machine is in dire need of repair, but the sheer energy and romance of the place is undeniable.

Carnegie Hall, situated on Seventh Avenue and 57th Street, opened in 1891 with a concert conducted by Tchaikovsky and has remained a legendary venue for serious musicians, both classical and popular. It was superbly restored in 1986, having narrowly escaped demolition. But none of this concerns us here.

However, diagonally across from Carnegie Hall, is a tall thirties building containing, on the fourteenth floor, a TV studio—currently the home of *Today In Fashion with Nathalie West.* This is a magazine program in which the perky and vivacious Nathalie West, a twenty-six-year-old blonde, covers fashion events and interviews designers and models.

She'd had them all: Vivienne Westwood, Jean-Paul Gaultier, Calvin Klein, Donna Karan, Cindy, Christy, and Naomi. Half the material was prerecorded and slotted into the half-hour show, which went out live.

It was 7:47 Eastern Standard Time, thirteen minutes before showtime. Nathalie West had been out of hair and makeup for about five minutes and was sitting at the assistant director's desk, going through her lines. Today she'd be interviewing Gianni Versace about the punk revival.

Nathalie's pet chihuahua, Poppy, was on her lap.

Poppy was one of the gimmicks of the show. She could be a pain in the ass. A few times she had started barking in the middle of an interview, and once she'd peed on a supermodel. But the survey guys said her demographics were great and the audience loved her, so Poppy stayed in the show.

The only person who didn't like Poppy was Nathalie's boyfriend, Jason Stone. Nathalie enjoyed a modern relationship with Jason, that is, it was more like a business relationship than a romance.

Jason was a hotshot reporter over at General News Networks. They were both on career fast tracks, saw each other when their schedules allowed, and looked good together at the schmooze fests they regularly attended.

In the control booth, the director was watching as a technician timed the Gianni Versace catwalk footage, with which they were going to open the show. On the floor, the floor manager was talking into his cell phone.

"Yeah? Make it snappy—we go out live in ten minutes." The floor manager's mouth dropped open. He couldn't believe what he was hearing.

"What?? The actual President? What do you mean cuttin' in? He can't cut in!"

Across the studio, Nathalie and Poppy looked up. They both had very good noses. They could smell when something was happening.

"Let me get this straight—you're saying that the President of the United States is cutting in on our show? I don't believe it!"

Nathalie picked up her phone.

Two blocks away at the GNN building, Jason Stone was sitting at his desk, feet up, hands behind his head, doing what he liked best: watching himself on TV. They were airing a news segment he'd done the day before—an interview with Chet Bickford, the Speaker of the House. At this moment, on TV, Jason was saying:

". . . That's the assessment of House Speaker Chet Bickford who launched a new verbal attack on President Dale, saying Mr. Dale is quote 'factually challenged' unquote."

"Hair looks good. I like the hair," Jason said to himself admiringly.

The phone rang. He picked it up, his eyes still glued to the screen.

"Yeah, Stone here—speak."

"Jason, hi, it's me, Nathalie!"

"Are you wearing a bra?"

"Shut up a second, this is big. President Dale is cutting in on my show today!"

Jason swung his feet off the desk and selected an M&M from the bowl by his computer terminal.

"That's absurd." He popped the M&M in his mouth. "Why would the President stoop to being on *Today In Fashion*?"

"He's interrupting everybody!" Nathalie was almost shouting. "It's some sort of emergency announcement or something."

Jason's feelings were hurt.

"What?" He clicked off the TV with his remote control. "This doesn't make any sense. He should be talking to us!"

Suddenly Jason's door flew open and Seymour, a reporter, poked his head in.

"The White House is coming on live!"

Seymour came in and sat down, followed by Albert Green, another reporter, and Ramon Rodriguez, an intern. Jason clicked the TV back on. It was showing the presidential seal.

"Okay, Nat, I'll call you later." Jason put the phone down and watched the screen.

The presidential seal faded out, to be replaced by the head and shoulders of James Dale. He was wearing a blue suit and sitting in an armchair, in front of a roaring fire.

"Good evening, my fellow Americans," he said.

More GNN reporters entered Jason's office and crowded around the TV. The room was charged with excitement.

"I apologize for interrupting your regular programs, but I have a very important announcement to make."

The reporters started shouting out theories.

"He freed the hostages!"

"He's not running for re-election!"

"They've balanced the budget!"

In Washington, D.C., in the Rose Room of the White House, President Dale addressed five TV cameras. Watching him were the First Lady, Jerry Ross, Professor Donald Kessler, General Jack Decker, General Bill Casey, a crowd of White House staff, and film crews from CBS, NBC, ABC, CNN, and Fox. Everyone was thrilled to be there.

"My friends, there are times . . ." drawled the President, "when the actors on the world's stage do not know that they are in a drama destined to alter the very foundations of our modern civilization. . . ."

Upstairs, in Taffy's bedroom, a White House waiter was decanting dinner from a trolley to a small table. He positioned the drink, which was covered by a napkin, next to the main dish, which was enclosed by an antique silver cover.

Taffy, the President's daughter, was sitting on her canopied bed (she'd devised the canopy herself), looking at her Kurt Cobain poster, which satisfyingly raped her mother's silk wallpapered wall. The TV was on and her father was speaking.

"How many of us know with absolute certainty that history is in the making? How many know the day? How many know the hour?"

She glanced at the waiter, setting up her dinner, and felt afraid. She didn't know how to behave with White House servants.

Taffy watched her father's face on TV. He was so familiar and yet so inaccessible. She loved him but he didn't belong to her. He belonged to everyone else.

"Many important things have happened to me in my life. My graduation from Princeton. The day Marsha said she would be my wife. My first car. The birth of our daughter, Taffy . . ."

Taffy cringed.

"Thanks, Dad!" she said sarcastically.

The waiter pushed out the rattling trolley and closed the door behind him.

"And the news I heard today ranks right up there. A powerful memory is in the making. Not just for me but for all of humankind."

Taffy crossed to the dinner table and sat down.

"Today an extraordinary discovery was made by the Hubble Space Telescope. A much criticized program which, I might add, has been solidly supported by this administration.

"Get to the POINT!" yelled Taffy at her father.

She'd had enough. She was sick of it. She wanted to kill them all—her father, her mother, her butt-kissing teachers, the slimeball politicians, the horrible kids at school who hated her.

Taffy lifted the dish cover, revealing a cheese and pepperoni pizza.

Standing at the crossing of two state highways in the middle of what seemed a huge and limitless plain of prairie, Perkinsville, Kansas, had a population of just over 2,000. Viewed from the middle of Main Street, the road to the north disappeared in a straight unbroken line off over the horizon. Turn around and look in the opposite direction, south, and it did exactly the same.

There was a red-brick church of the 1920s on one corner, and a 1960s First National Bank on the other—and a gas station, a donut shop, Ace Video Rentals, Loretta's Cafe, Parker's Flower and Gift, a pharmacy, a supermarket, and Judy's Ladieswear.

In side roads off Main Street, were a neoclassic four-story courthouse and a public library building, and trim rows of houses with mailboxes in front of them. Not far away, beyond the town's edge were wind-rippled wheat fields—grazing land with herds of cattle—and, here and there, isolated farms among clumps of trees.

In the donut shop, named Bob's Donuts, nothing much was happening. The place was empty except for Chucky who was nursing a cold cup of coffee and pretending to read a newspaper.

The sheriff of Perkinsville had called Chucky "one big no-good vagrant bum."

Behind the counter, Maria, a depressed Hispanic woman who'd moved here from Deerfield seven years before, wiped the counter very slowly, as if she were barely alive. Things were slow in Perkinsville.

Out of sight, at the back of the shop, surrounded by metal trays of raw donuts, was a skinny young man of nineteen in a Kurt Cobain T-shirt. This was Richie Norris, the manager. For the last three hours he'd been smoking joints and watching the store's ancient black-and-white TV—sitting on an old car seat taken from his grandma's derelict '64 Ford Falcon.

Too stoned to get up, he concentrated on the talking face of President Dale.

"The data from the Hubble telescope was decoded, then analyzed by the most powerful computers at MIT. The verifications are complete. The images are irrefutable. We are entering the dawn of a new era."

"Go for it, dude!" yelled Richie.

Over at the counter, Maria lifted her head and waited. A few moments passed and, hearing no more, she returned to her unhurried wiping of the counter.

Meanwhile, in Las Vegas, in the crowded sports bar of the Luxor Hotel, everyone was riveted to the TV screens. These screens usually showed different sporting events, but now they all displayed the same image: President James Dale.

"The frame enlargements provide an astounding sight . . ." he said, giving an actor's pause. The audience of the sports bar held its collective breath.

". . . a large fleet of vehicles, which can best be described as flying saucers. These flying saucers have come from the planet Mars and, at their current course and speed, will be entering Earth's orbit in approximately sixteen hours."

Everyone gasped. Larry Bava, the casino manager, couldn't believe it. Was this some kind of gag? Cindy, the pretty waitress in the costume of an Ancient Egyptian slave girl (except for the push-up bra), almost dropped her tray of drinks.

"Holy heck!" she exclaimed.

Joe Weinberg, a Vegas lawyer with a drinking *and* a gambling problem, looked up from the craps table. Where was everybody?

"Hey! Am I the only one shooting craps here?! Send them bones back!" he yelled at the dealer. "Come on! *Today!*"

A mile away, near the golf course, in one of the most upscale homes in Las Vegas, Barbara Land was giddy with excitement.

"Martians! This is great! This is great!" she cried.

On TV, the President was saying: "We don't know what they want, or if they intend to contact us. But we sincerely hope we will have the opportunity to meet with them."

"Please come to Earth. Please!" begged Barbara. "Please! Please! Please! We *need* you!"

While this was happening, her husband was in his office—NOT watching TV. Art's office was one of the first rooms in the new Galaxy Hotel to be finished, and was a sight to behold. He had designed it himself. Italian muralists had painted images of gods and goddesses, planets and stars on every available surface. In a large alcove, suspended from the eighteen-foot ceiling was a massive globe of the Earth. Outside the giant windows, Las Vegas lay at his feet. This was the office of a conqueror, which is exactly how Art saw himself.

On a table was a scale model of the Galaxy—perfect in every detail—even down to little scale models of valet-parking guys. A sign on the tabletop display said: *Art Land's* GALAXY HOTEL AND CASINO.

Art, dressed in a black cowboy shirt with white piping and nickel wing tips, black jeans, longhorn belt buckle, and calfskin cowboy boots studded with Mexican silver conchoes, was on the phone, talking to his banker.

We're stalled down here till this new financing comes through, understand? I can't lay no pipes for the Jacuzzis. All the stuff is sitting in some railroad siding somewheres. But don't worry about it, I got people coming in. I got people coming in from Switzerland and Texas and Saudi Arabia. Hey! Everybody wants to be a part of this. The Galaxy is gonna be world class. So, how's my credit?"

In New York, in the General News Networks building on Seventh Avenue, chaos reigned. Only a few were still watching the TVs—most were running around and bumping into each other and yelling out demands. In his office, Jason barked orders into his phone.

"See if we can get patched into NASA! And get me some man-in-the-street reactions! And somebody track down Carl Sagan!"

On TV, the President's voice changed pitch, dipping down into those thrilling chocolate tones.

"I feel this is a perfect inauguration to the twenty-first century. The last century saw two of the worst wars in human history, but also saw the dropping of borders and, give or take a few problems like Cuba, the extending of friendship in all directions. People want peace. And the duty of government is to give it to them."

Two blocks away, on the *Today In Fashion* set,

Nathalie West was having a frenzied, impromptu conference with her "team."

"We *have* to change the order of the show. Do a piece on the Martians! What do they look like? What do they wear? And we can slot it in right after the leg-waxing thing."

"Good idea," said the director.

In Washington, D.C., in the White House, upstairs in her room, Taffy ate pizza and watched her dad on TV.

"Communism has fallen, and now there is no East or West—just us. We have become one planet. And soon we will become one solar system.

"It is profoundly moving to know that there is intelligent life out there," said the President.

"Glad they got it somewhere," said Taffy.

In the Rose Room, bathed in the TV lights, President Dale was nearing the end of his speech. The First Lady and Jerry Ross watched him proudly.

Camera #1 pushed in slowly on the President's face. He resisted the urge to blink and gazed at the lens, eyes glowing with pride and emotion.

"Our lives and our world will never feel the same again. Good night and God bless you all."

There was a long moment of silence. The President didn't move. Then the director stepped forward, pulled off his earphones and said: "Cut! It's a wrap!"

The small audience in the Rose Room burst into applause. President Dale couldn't resist a smile. He knew he'd made a hit.

Chapter 6

'Tis the hour when white-hors'd day
Chases Night, her mares, away;
And the Gates of Dawn, so they say,
Phoebus opes.

And I gather that the Queen
May be uniformly seen,
Should the weather be serene,
On the slopes.

—Anonymous

The great golden orb, to which we owe all life, peeped over the Atlantic and besprinkled the land with its cold, virgin rays. Dark turned to gray, turned to color along the wiggly coasts, the dockyards, the roads, the islands, the waterways, the monuments, the bridges, and myriad buildings of Gotham. It was sunup in New York City.

Downtown, on Canal Street, the smell of old

gasoline mixed with garbage and Chinese food was flavored with the crisp and salty morning air. A truck with lettering on the side thundered past, bouncing noisily over the manhole covers and those large metal plates they like to cover patches of road with in Manhattan.

The truck approached a closed-up newsstand. The side door slammed open and a pair of hands threw something out. Thump! A pile of tied-together newspapers landed on the sidewalk—and the truck sped on. It was the *New York Times*. On the front page was a picture of the Martian fleet and the headline: EXISTENCE OF INTERPLANETARY LIFE CONFIRMED.

Suddenly there was the roar of a second truck. Whap! A second pile of newspapers landed on the sidewalk. This time it was the *New York Post*, with the very same picture on its front page. The headline simply: MARTIANS!!!!

A few hours later, in the kitchen of Jason Stone's Upper West Side apartment, the famous media couple were having breakfast, both dressed in baggy white pajamas. Jason was eating Mueslix with fruit and nonfat milk, while Nathalie devoured pancakes drenched in syrup.

"Are you sure you don't want any? I can make some more."

"No thanks," said Jason, absorbed in the Martian story in the *Times*.

Nathalie went back to reading her copy of the *Post*.

"Wow," said Jason. "This is intense."

The phone rang, and Poppy, the chihuahua, leapt off Nathalie's lap and ran, yelping hysterically, around the room. Poppy went into crazy-insane barking mode every time the phone rang, which was useful if you were in the garden and couldn't hear the phone in the house, but as both Nathalie and Jason lived in small New York apartments, this was not applicable.

"Hey, Poppy, shut up! Shut up!!"

Jason grabbed the cordless phone. "Stone here."

The dog stopped barking and Jason turned, blank-faced, to Nathalie.

"It's for you."

"Oh yeah?"

Nathalie licked her fingertips, wiped them on her pajamas, and held out her hand. Jason gave her the phone and resumed his seat.

"Yeah? Yeah sure," she said, in her sexy early-morning voice. "I can be there at eleven—no problem."

"Okay, love you, bye!" She pressed the hangup button, put the phone down on the table, and returned to her paper.

Jason looked at her with irritation. "So . . . ?"

"That was Brian from the show. He wants me to, I don't know, go interview some guy or something."

"Oh yeah? What, some fashion moron?"

"No, this guy's an expert on Martians. He's that famous professor, you know the one. Kessler—that's his name . . . David Kessler, I think."

"Not *Donald* Kessler?" He looked at her, dumfounded.

"Could be. Yeah. You know—the scientist."

Poppy jumped into her lap.

"But this is crazy. GNN should be getting him!"

Nathalie hated it when that whining sound entered Jason's voice. She flicked him an icy look.

"I can't help it if your people are too slow. Isn't that right, Poppy?" She caressed the dog with her long, manicured forefinger, right under the collar—just where she liked it. Poppy wriggled with pleasure and seemed to smile. Jason seemed to sulk.

Main Street, Perkinsville, runs east to west. All the streets running across, from north to south, are named after American Presidents. You've got Washington Street, Jefferson Street, Lincoln Street, Grant Street, and so on. It was the great idea of the town commissioners, a few years back, to change the names of the streets so as to give the town more civic pride. The way it was before, the streets were just plain First, Second, Third, Fourth through Tenth. But that meant it was too easy to find your way around. Now you've got to have a bachelor's degree in history and know whether Monroe comes before Jefferson or Grant precedes Garfield. Neat idea, huh?

On the north side of Main you get the smarter residences. These belong to the folks with money. Some of them have got satellite dishes on their front lawns. Satellite dishes are the latest status symbol in Perkinsville. The wives say: "What do we need a hundred channels for?" Their husbands say: "To get all the sports channels, honey, that's why." But what they really mean is they want Channel seventy-six, the one that has the late-night blue movies.

On the south side of Main is where the poorer folks are situated. If you go six blocks you get to the railroad and the reservoir and the trailer parks. Just beyond that is the interstate highway. They say, in the old days, when the railroad was more active, this neighborhood was prosperous, with a store and a school and a post office, but now it's pretty run-down.

Richie Norris, the skinny runt who works at Bob's Donuts, lives here in a big sixty-foot trailer, which he shares with his mother, father, and brother; though his brother is in the army, so he isn't home much.

It was a small trailer park, no more than twenty-five trailers, off a dirt road that led one way into town and the other way to the interstate. People parked their cars any which way they happened to feel like, which always made it look like some emergency had just happened. But nothing happened usually, except disputes.

Richie's father, Glenn, a man who thought Velveeta was gourmet cheese, was always getting into disputes with the neighbors. Glenn was fifty-five and worked at a gas station and (like General Decker) was a Vietnam vet.

It was 9:37 A.M. and the Norris family had just finished breakfast.

Sue-Ann Norris, Richie's mother, was reading the *Weekly World News*. There was a story featuring several photos of burning cattle and the headline: KENTUCKY FRIED CATTLE! Underneath one of the photos was the caption: "Aliens did this to my cows!" Sue-Ann was interested in cows, having been around them all her life, being as her father was a cowhand—and she had followed the many alien sightings announced in the press over the years with genuine concern. As time went by, there seemed to be more and more UFO sightings, alien abductions, and government cover-ups. It looked to her like it was building up to something. It was very worrying. But, well, cows—that was a new twist. Aliens and cows in the same story was certainly very interesting.

Slumped in the corner on the built-in couch was Grandma Norris, a line of spittle running from her mouth to her chin like a snail track. Grandma was eighty-eight years old and missing a few marbles. She wasn't Sue-Ann's mother, oh no, *her* mother was as sharp as a tack. No, she was Glenn's mother—and she was senile. They'd put her in a retirement home, where the Asian nurses looked after her real well. But sometimes Glenn liked to have her come over. She'd come over yesterday; Richie had brought her in the pickup. And everybody had gotten too drunk to drive her back, so she'd stayed the night, sleeping on the couch. She was fine. She liked being with the family.

Sue-Ann leaned across and wiped the spittle from her chin with a Kleenex.

"You okay, Grandma?"

Grandma continued to gaze into the middle distance, a crooked smile on her face.

On TV it was the News. The news anchor, the one who looked like a turkey with a toupee, was talking about the Martians:

"They are continuing to stay in a holding pattern in orbit around the earth. The latest count is 2,678 space vehicles—and, as you can see, they sure do make an impressive sight."

Behind the newscaster was a screen on which Hubble Space Telescope pictures of the Martian armada were projected.

"We've had a lot of calls here at the station, most of them concerned about one thing. Are the Martians friendly? Well, frankly, we don't know yet, but the statement issued this morning by the Pentagon says that the situation is under control and there is no cause for alarm. People are advised to go about their daily business in the usual way that they do."

But no one took any notice of the TV, they hardly ever did, unless somebody turned it off. Richie was watching his older brother, Billy-Glenn, assembling the component parts of a rifle at high speed. Billy-Glenn, twenty-four, was kneeling on the floor, shirtless, in just his boxer shorts, a blindfold over his eyes. Glenn Norris, the father, was timing him with a stopwatch.

"Finished!"

Billy-Glenn yanked off his blindfold and grinned at his dad. "How long?"

Glenn examined his watch with grave dignity. "One minute fifty-seven seconds."

"Hot damn! Didn't I tell you under two minutes?"

"You did, son."

Glenn Norris's face twitched; it was a sign he was pleased.

Richie was leaning on the wall, feeling like a loser. He decided to get some donuts from the refrigerator outside.

The dog, a German shepherd named Prince, was chained to a stake in the ground. He looked up expectantly as Richie came out.

"Hello, Prince, how ya doing? You want a donut?"

Prince dragged his chain over to Richie, wagging his tail.

Richie opened the big old Westinghouse refrigerator, which they kept outside so as to save space, and took out a white cardboard box.

"You like these, huh?"

He took out a glazed donut and held it out. The dog swallowed it in two chomps. Prince ate just like an alligator—no chewing.

"Okay, boy."

Richie gave him a couple of pats and went back inside.

On TV the Martian news continued. A balding pundit in suit, tie, and spectacles was speaking: "Scientific observations of the spacecraft reveal that Martian technology is far ahead of ours and therefore indicates a civilization more advanced than our own. What this tells us is that the pilots of these vehicles are highly developed and enlightened beings, who indeed may show the human race many things to its benefit."

"Hey, Mom, you want a donut?" said Richie.

"How old are they?" she queried.

"Fresh baked Monday."

She shot him a look of reproach.

"Goddammit, Richie, that's six days ago!"

Richie felt that familiar feeling of failure, but at least everyone was looking at him—his dad, his brother, even Grandma, though what *she* was seeing was probably someone else. Sue-Ann sensed a small wrinkle in her stomach that still had a little stretch left.

"Okay, gimme two."

Richie passed around the box. They all took one.

"This Martian thing is awesome, huh?" Richie said sociably.

"Has anyone seen my Muffy?" asked Grandma.

Everyone ignored her.

Glenn took a donut.

"Your brother's gonna volunteer."

"Soon as I get back to the base," said Billy-Glenn.

"Volunteer for what?" asked Richie.

"Martian detail."

"Cool."

Glenn chewed thoughtfully. A thought was forming.

"You know what?" he said. "You know what?" he said again, looking around at Sue-Ann and Richie and Billy-Glenn.

"If any of them Martians come around here, I'm gonna *kick their butts!*"

"He will too," said Sue-Ann.

Everyone nodded at the rightness of this and Glenn relaxed back in his recliner.

Las Vegas seems all wrong in the daytime. Sometimes small bands of tourists venture, uncertainly, out on to the streets, but not for long. They squint into the desert sun, get uncomfortable, then hurry back into the air-conditioned, velvet night of the casinos.

On Yucca Street, a tall wire fence surrounded the vast corner lot where the Galaxy Hotel and Casino was being constructed.

Beside the entrance to the site stood a large billboard displaying an artist's rendering of the finished hotel, complete with palm trees and swimming pools—all tastefully airbrushed. Large letters trumpeted: ART LAND'S GALAXY HOTEL AND CASINO—OPENING SUMMER 2003!

The main building was almost finished. Now it was at the plumbing and wiring stage. They were scheduled to start on the interiors next week.

In Art's resplendent office, two painters were putting finishing touches to the filigree patterns on the gold-painted woodwork around the bar.

Art stood at the center window, gazing down at the Las Vegas strip. He was on the phone to an investor in Los Angeles. They'd been talking about the Martians, but Art wanted to get the subject around to his hotel.

"Listen, pal, I was thinking Martians before there even *were* Martians! You seen the brochure? We got a five-million-dollar space ride and a whole building full of that Virtual Reality shit. This is gonna be the best hotel in Vegas!"

In Washington, D.C., at the exclusive Georgetown Golf Course, General Decker yelled "Fore!" and swung his favorite nine-iron through a perfect parabolic arc. Whack! The ball rose high in the air.

Colonel Korn, Brigadier Eberhardie, and the three black caddies (requisitioned from the barracks), watched the ball arch slowly over the fairway, sail down, bounce twice, and roll to a stop ten yards from the hole.

Hmm. Not bad, thought Decker.

Korn's ball was at the edge of the green and Eberhardie's was in the rough. Decker thrust his driver out at arm's length and his caddie ran up and took it.

"Lucky," appraised the brigadier.

"Lucky, my ass," said Decker.

As they set off toward the green, Eberhardie knew this was the right moment to ask the question.

"So, Jack, what'd the President say?"

Decker's steel-blue eyes flashed.

"You wanna know what he said? I'll tell you what he said. He said: 'Peace and Love. Open the gates and let the invaders in!'"

His two golfing comrades had expected this but, still, they were shocked.

Colonel Korn shook his head.

"George Bush would never let this happen."

The brigadier grunted in agreement.

Decker stopped walking, put his hands on his hips, and looked at the turf by his feet, as if, somehow, the answer lay there. His two colleagues watched. Something was brewing. Decker had been preoccupied all morning. The caddies, traipsing behind, came to a ragged halt.

"What's up, Jack?" asked Eberhardie.

Decker stuck out his chin and his bald, bullet-head gleamed in the sun. "I'll tell you what's up," he growled. "I am not going to give America away without a fight!" He glanced sideways at the caddies and gestured for the military men to come closer.

"Look," he said, lowering his voice, "without going through official channels, I want to put the Reserves on alert. What do you say? Let's beef up the troops . . . just in case."

Chapter 7

Lord, make me an instrument of Your peace.
Where there is hatred let me sow love;
Where there is injury, pardon;
Where there is doubt, faith;
Where there is despair, hope;
Where there is darkness, light;
Where there is sadness, joy.

—Saint Francis of Assisi

It has long been considered ironic that the capital city of the United States—sometimes referred to as "Paris on the Potomac"—contains some of the worst slums in the country.

These ugly, depressed, and scary-looking areas are inhabited mostly by angry African-Americans.

Indeed, there are slaves in America today. There are at least two million illegal immigrants living in the U.S. These "illegals" have no civil rights and are exploited by employers who pay them slave wages.

Henry Gibbon, the famous historian, observed that all civilizations were built on slavery. The Chinese dynasties, Egypt, Greece, Rome, the Holy Roman Empire, the Spanish Empire, the British Empire, even Australia—all had a slave class. Russia had slavery until Czar Nicholas freed the serfs in 1888. And in Europe, slavery gradually changed its form over several centuries of Peasants' Revolts, evolving into the class system that exists today. So African-Americans are not the only group with slave ancestors.

Where does the anger come from? Is it because of segregation—because of the "Jim Crow" laws in the South? Some people can still remember the "white only" rest rooms, the "black only" schools—the humiliating apartheid that existed in parts of America right up until the 1960s. But there is no apartheid in the U.S. today—at least, not officially, not legally.

Maybe African-Americans are angry because of discrimination? The word 'discrimination,' which usually means to 'use good judgment' (be discriminating), has a negative spin when used in the context of race. It has come to mean a prejudicial act against the African-American, who is "discriminated against" because of the color of his skin. But then, does not this predominantly

Caucasian society also "discriminate against" Filipinos, Mexicans, Chinese, Arabs . . . in fact, all non-Caucasians?

And what about the Native Americans? They were robbed of their land and systematically murdered, as government policy. Killing Indians was not even a crime until 1892 because the government did not recognize them as human beings. After 1892, Indians were given limited rights, and classified as "resident aliens." But it wasn't until 1922 that Indians were given the vote. The black man had the vote in 1846. So, why aren't Native Americans more angry?

What is different about blacks? Are they more sensitive to pain than others? Are they less inclined to suppress their emotions? Whatever the reason, their anger is counterproductive. Raw anger can be addictive. You can get release and power in that choleric rush of energy, but it evaporates quickly and never produces a good result. If anger is not channeled, it is useless. Rage alone solves no problems, and in the slums of Washington, there are a lot of unsolved problems.

Driving her city bus through the ghetto, Louise Williams, the beautiful, fortyish ex-wife of Luxor-greeter Byron Williams, had some problems of her own. The main one, right now, was Sheldon.

"Just one date! What's it gonna hurt?"

Sheldon was leaning over her while she was steering the bus through a busy intersection.

"Back in the bus, Sheldon, or I'm gonna stop and kick your ass out!" she yelled.

Sheldon was a regular passenger. She'd been in a good mood one day and had flirted with him. Now she regretted it.

Sheldon was a white postal worker who thought he had "personality."

"Please, please, Louise, I'm on my knees!"

"Back in the bus!"

"Come on, baby, you look so foxy in that uniform! Tight butts drive me nuts!"

"Back in the bus *now*!"

Sheldon smirked, covering his failure with an attitude of mock triumph. "I'll see you later," he said, and went and sat down.

Two blocks away, Louise's sons, Cedric, fifteen, and Neville, thirteen, were in the open store front of a general store, only a couple of steps from the pavement. They were playing a lurid video game named *Flesh-Eaters*.

Neville watched as his brother rapid-fired an electronic gun at little Pac-Men who were eating the flesh off the body of a handsome blond lifeguard dressed in swim trunks. Cedric blasted the Pac-Men off the lifeguard's body and every hit produced an electronic scream and scored ten points. Cedric held the highest score on this machine. He was an expert marksman, with lightning reflexes.

Cedric and Neville were playing hooky from school, which Cedric often did when it was Mr. Portman's class. He taught geography and was so shortsighted he couldn't see as far as the back of the class where Cedric sat.

Neville, who was two years younger, had a free period followed by Math. He had planned to go back over the wall in time for the Math class, but now he wanted to try and beat Cedric's score. He knew he was going to get in trouble because the dragon who taught Math, was way fascist—but, hell, they couldn't throw him out, could they?

In the bus, the last of the passengers dropped the bus fare into the chute and Louise pressed the door-close button. The bus doors hissed shut. Everything was clear, so she let out the clutch and pulled into the traffic. There was nothing up ahead. She'd have an open run to the stop light. She relaxed. What was the time? She checked her watch—4:45—only one more hour to quitting time. Shit! What were *they* doing here? She slammed on the brakes. "Excuse me, folks, we gotta make a unscheduled stop!" She punched the door button. The bus doors snapped open and out she flew.

Cedric and Neville looked round.

"It's Mama," said Neville.

"What!?" said Cedric.

"What you doing here?" she shouted. "Why aren't you in school?" Louise rushed upon them like an irate elk.

"I *said* what you doing here?!"

"Class was canceled," lied Cedric.

"Don't you lie to me! Class wasn't canceled!" Louise grabbed Cedric's ear and twisted it hard.

"Ow! That hurts!"

"Good. Neville, come here."

"For what?" said Neville, backing away nervously.

"Come here. It's all right, I'm not gonna hurt you." She was gripping and twisting Cedric's ear so hard that tears were coming out of his eyes.

"Let go of his ear!" cried Neville.

"And then you'll come over here?"

"Yes," said Neville, very apprehensive.

"Okay." Louise let go of Cedric's ear and crooked her finger at Neville. "Come here."

Neville approached her warily. Faster than a whip, she slapped him in the face!

"Owwww!"

The bus passengers were at the bus windows,

watching. Sheldon gazed at Louise with admiration.

"You think it's smart to cut school? Do you? Do you?"

"No, Mama," said Neville guiltily, one side of his face a bright crimson.

"Do you?" she said to Cedric.

"No, Mama."

"No, Mama, 'cause it's dumb. You're gonna flunk. You're gonna get in trouble. You're gonna go to jail. What did I do? I been a good mother to you, ain't I? Ain't I?"

"Yes, Mama," they both said together.

"So why can't you be good? Why can't you be good? You smoking crack?"

"No, Mama," said Cedric.

"Get on the bus," she yelled. "Go on, get on the bus! You make me sick!" She slapped, pushed, and kicked them on to the bus and followed after them. "Now, sit down and shut up!"

As the kids headed sheepishly for the back of the bus, the passengers, led by Sheldon, broke into applause.

"Okay, that's enough of that," said Louise, resuming her seat. She closed the doors and put the bus in gear.

Across the street, three prostitutes watched the bus thunder past. One of them, a pretty redhead named Dolly, was surreptitiously eating toothpaste from a tube. It's a strange habit, but it perks you up if you're feeling tired, and Dolly was tired. She'd been working since nine the previous evening, and the crystal meth was wearing off.

"Hey, Dolly," said the youngest of the three hookers. "Would you screw a man from Mars?"

Dolly twisted back the top of the toothpaste tube, and replaced it in her purse. "Yeah, but no kissin' on the lips."

A sleek black limo pulled up a few yards down the street. The girls ran over, and the back window slid down. Dolly peered in the window and saw a man sitting inside. He looked all right. He looked rich and clean.

"Hey, baby, you want a date?" said Dolly, batting her eyes.

"Sounds good," said Jerry Ross. "The stress at work is unbelievable." He smiled, leaned over, and opened the door.

"The greatest of evils and the worst of crimes is poverty."
—George Bernard Shaw
Major Barbara

Deep in the entrails of the Luxor Casino, surrounded by gamblers and onlookers, Joe Weinberg was shooting craps. Since he'd left his buddies at "Nudes On Ice," he'd had three cognacs, some weird cocktail one of those slut waitresses had suckered him into, five double Scotches, and a bunch of beers.

"I'm hot! I'm hot as a pistol! I'm sizzling! Come on, baby! Do it for me! Yeah!" He threw the dice. Nine! He won again!

"Hey, how about that?" he said to a glassy-eyed blonde from Texas who was sitting next to him.

She didn't reply. She was there with her husband.

Joe Weinberg was a litigation lawyer. He was paid $500 an hour to argue with people. It came naturally. In fact, he'd even argue with people for free. His gimlet eyes watched the dealer count out his winning chips. He didn't trust this dealer. Actually, he didn't trust anyone. His job proved to him, daily, that everyone will cheat you, if they think they can get away with it.

Cindy, the pretty cocktail waitress, came over to the table, tottering on her high heels. Her large breasts gleamed like soft, honey-colored cantaloupes as she took the drinks orders.

Joe didn't even notice her. He was watching the poker-faced dealer.

"Excuse me, would you like a drink?"

Joe looked up. He was a short man and his face almost collided with Cindy's amazing boobs.

"Huh?"

"We're running a special tonight," Cindy bubbled. "It's called The Martian, and it's creme de menthe and Bombay gin in a souvenir plastic flying saucer!"

"Oh yeah?" said Joe, recovering his aplomb, "Well, it sounds disgusting. Gimme a Scotch." Something was happening in his peripheral vision. The dealer was moving something. "Hey! What are you doing with that chip? I saw that! You trying to cheat me?"

The dealer looked at him with tired eyes. He hated guys like this. All he was doing was neatening some chips that had spilled over.

"Place your bets, please," he said.

Joe turned to the glassy-eyed blonde from Texas, and grinned.

"Hey, baby, how you doing? You want a chip?"

In another part of the casino, Byron Williams, looking ridiculous in his pharoah outfit with its floppy headdress, was searching for Mr. Bava. He'd come early to work in order to speak to him.

The Nevada Electric Company was going to cut off Byron's electricity for nonpayment. He could cover it, but only if he used the child-support money he was planning to send to Louise for the kids. He was trying to get back in Louise's good books, so the last thing he wanted was to be late with the check—and payday was a whole two weeks off. Even though he'd quit drinking and had learned to be economical by writing down all his purchases in a little notebook, he was still getting into these cash crunches. He badly needed a raise.

He spotted the casino manager over by the mah-jongg tables.

"Mr. Bava, could we speak in private?"

"No, I gotta watch the floor. Whatdya want, Byron?"

Byron paused, he wanted to say this right.

"Well, you know, I'm supporting a family back east . . ."

"I thought you were divorced."

"Well, I am, but I'm trying to take care of them. Anyway, times are kind of lean . . . and I was wondering if I could get a raise?"

The casino manager looked at him as if he was a not-very-interesting stain on the carpet.

"Out of the question."

"But, Mr. Bava . . . I'm an asset to this hotel. People like me . . ."

"Don't push it, Byron, okay? I can get Leon Spinks or Buster Douglas for the same money—maybe less." He glanced at his watch. "You'd better get to your station. You're on in five minutes."

The casino manager walked away. Byron turned, feeling lonely. Where were his friends? Where was his love? Where were his children?

Somehow, he'd made a mess of his life and time had run out. He was too old for second chances. No one gave a damn about a middle-aged, washed-up, has-been black man—even if he *had* renounced the Devil and turned virtuous. Nobody cared about virtue; all they cared about was success.

"Nobody wants you when you're down and out" were the words to the song, and they said it right. When you're down, people kick you. Jesus Christ was a wonderful man. He tried to make people understand, forgive, have compassion, help the needy, admire virtue. But people never will. Jesus was a dreamer. He tried. He tried so hard. He even got himself killed trying. But He failed.

Chapter 9

There is nothing wrong with your
television set. Do not attempt to
adjust the picture. We are
controlling transmission.

—The Outer Limits

In midtown Manhattan, a strange thickness had entered the atmosphere. It was as if the air itself anticipated something unpleasant. But this mood is not uncommon in the Big Apple, where lurid and monstrous events happen daily. New York is nothing if not dramatic, which is why New Yorkers love it.

In the directing booth of the *Today In Fashion* TV studio, the director and the chief mixer sat at the control desk, looking through the wide concave window at the studio floor below. Beyond the three cameras, on the small, jazzy set, Michelle, the makeup person, was taking the shine off Professor Donald Kessler's forehead with a number three powder brush. Next to Kessler, on the pistachio-green vinyl couch, sat Nathalie West. She crossed her legs. She uncrossed them. She couldn't get comfortable.

Beneath the smell of the Professor's newly applied TV makeup, she detected an acrid tweediness—a mixture of expensive wool, pipe tobacco, and eau de cologne. It reminded her, vividly, of her history teacher from her freshman year in high school—Mr. Baxter, the first man she had ever loved.

Her mind swam back to those days at Scotsdale High; the brutality of the boys, the cruelty of the girls, and the godlike perfection of Mr. Baxter. He was her lighthouse in a stormy sea. Not only was he good-looking in an older-man kind of way, not only did he know everything, not only was he tender and kind, but also, (unlike the other teachers) he didn't come on to her. At night, in her little bedroom, she would shock herself with elaborate fantasies involving Mr. Baxter. She never told a living soul about her unusual infatuation. Her friends would have found it totally gross.

Years later, Nathalie confided her schoolgirl passion for her history teacher to her therapist. This led to six months of expensive conversation regarding her relationship (or not) with her father.

Nathalie's father, Bill West, was an enigmatic guy. At the age of nineteen, Bill West stopped talking. He got a job as a deep-sea diver, working for treasure hunters in the Caribbean. At first, people were disconcerted, even intimidated, by his silence, but he was a good diver and, for someone who didn't speak, he had an uncommonly benevolent presence.

Bill West met Nathalie's mother in a hospital, after a broken diving-cage cable tore out the ligaments of his left arm. Linda, an RN, had always been attracted to damaged men. Her father had been a tyrant and her childhood was a voyage through persecution, self-abnegation, and martyrdom. She empathized, nay, fully identified with the oppressed, the crushed, the tormented, which was probably why she was attracted to nursing.

When she saw the beautiful, young Bill West, his arm torn from its socket, and a deeper pain beneath the physical pain in his eyes, she fell in love. They were married a year later.

At the wedding ceremony, when the minister said: "Do you take this woman to be your lawful wedded wife?" Linda had Bill hold up a card on which was written: "I do."

It took Linda five years of steadfast loving devotion to get Bill to speak.

So, for the first four years of Nathalie's young life, her father never said a word, and after that, she wished he hadn't. For, when Bill began to talk, he did nothing but cuss. He was diagnosed with Tourette's syndrome.

Nathalie's therapist suggested that her father was a father in name only; that some unknown trauma had decided him not to engage with the world; that he had replaced one barrier (silence) with another (cussing); and that her crush on Mr. Baxter was an expression of her need for the masculine, parental approbation denied her as a child.

Now, at the age of twenty-six, Nathalie was a TV celebrity, the host of her own show. Once a week, seven million viewers gave her a lot of approbation . . . but it wasn't enough. Her boyfriend, Jason Stone, one of the best-looking and most popular journalists on TV, gave her lots of approbation . . . but it wasn't enough. Her little dog, Poppy, loved her unconditionally . . . but it wasn't enough.

However, now, gazing at Professor Donald Kessler, she felt a tingling sensation at the center of her being, and a sudden, joyous awareness of the possibility of fulfillment. But she knew nothing would happen. Donald Kessler was one of the most intelligent men in the world—with more letters after his name than a FedEx tracking code. Whereas she, Nathalie, had never finished high school.

In the control booth, the director surveyed his prize-guest, Professor Donald Kessler, and flicked an excited glance at Liam, the chief mixer. "This show's gonna get a helluva rating!" he said.

"You bet!" said Liam.

On the TV monitors a catwalk fashion show was playing. It was the new Donna Karan collection. In the booth, the assistant director was timing it. Nathalie's commentary had been written. Maybe they could fit it in after the second commercial break?

On the jazzy *Today In Fashion* set, Nathalie stroked her chihuahua and chatted with her special guest. She didn't fully understand what Kessler was saying, but it sounded wonderful.

"So you see, Miss West," he said. "Wittgenstein was right, it all depends on the language you choose to employ. And in certain circumstances, the proposition that two and two equal five is entirely legitimate."

Nathalie looked into his slate-gray eyes.

"Call me Nathalie," she said, her voice coming out weaker than it was meant to.

Donald Kessler was a human tortoise. He

liked to stay inside the safety of his shell. But Nathalie West affected him.

"And you, uh, do, please, call me Donald."

It has long been observed that men and women are different. Men, for example, are attracted to secondary sexual characteristics. These are: hair, skin, eyes, lips, neck, shoulders, breasts, stomach, hips, arms, hands, ass, pubis, thighs, the small curve at the top of the inner thighs, calves, feet, toes, the curve of the instep . . . in fact, any part of the woman's body is an incitement to passion. Men are stimulated visually.

Women, on the other hand, are more mysterious. They are attracted to energies. These energies may be conveyed visually, but they can equally be conveyed by the voice, body-posture, smell and, above all, psychic vibration.

Much has been spoken of female intuition. It has long been noted that female intuition exists in order to interpret the needs of the infant. A baby cannot speak, so how does the mother know what the baby wants? Nature has provided a sixth sense to cope with this. The woman can use this sixth sense (or intuition) for other purposes, such as in the selecting of a mate. This is why men, who generally do not possess a sixth sense, are so clueless.

Two years ago, Donald Kessler had gone to

visit a colleague at MIT, a gerontologist. It was when they were studying the part genetics played in the aging process.

When Donald came in, his colleague was taking a break; resting his mind by watching a fashion program on television. To be polite, Donald watched the show with him, and was fascinated by the beauty of the presenter. She was everything he was not—young, blond, and bursting with health. She was like sunshine and fresh spring water. He found himself musing sadly on the certainty that he would never know a girl such as this.

Since then, as a sort of hobby, he had followed the career of the presenter. Whenever he saw her picture in a magazine, he would buy it. And he became a secret viewer of *Today In Fashion with Nathalie West*.

"Actually, I've admired your show for some time," averred Donald shyly. Nathalie couldn't believe it. Was he telling the truth? Why would a man like him watch her show? It seemed incredible. But, instinctively, she knew Donald Kessler was not a man who lied.

"Really? You like my work?" She felt herself blushing.

"Yes," he said, blushing, too. "Very much!"

The assistant director was signaling at them. He held up five fingers. "Coming out of commercial," he said in a loud voice. "Five, four . . . three . . . two . . ." He pointed to Nathalie. She spun perkily to camera.

"Welcome back! This is Nathalie West on *Today In Fashion* and today we're doing something completely different." She gave a big, deep-throated smile. "Hey, the summer collections can wait, okay? No, seriously, today we're doing something serious."

The camera panned across to Donald Kessler.

"Today, we're talking to Professor Donald Kessler, the chairman of the American Academy of Astronomics, uh, Astronautics . . . Did I get that right, Professor?"

"Yes, that's right," said Donald nervously.

Nathalie was exhilarated by the feeling of control she had over this idyllic man. He may be a great scientist, but it was *her* show. She'd already decided to keep the interview going after the next commercial.

"So, Professor, let me hit you with this: Isn't it kinda weird that we sent a space probe to Mars and didn't even find anyone?"

Donald looked at her. Maybe it was the bright TV lights, maybe it was the unfamiliarity of the situation, but he was dazzled.

"Not really, uh, Nathalie, because we didn't go into the canals."

Nathalie gave him a frankly sexual look. What

had he said? Canals? Had she caught him looking at her breasts?

In Washington, in the White House, the President, the First Lady, and Rusty, their golden retriever, were watching the Kessler interview on TV. President Dale had great faith in the professor. He could still remember chemistry class in school—boy, was it hard! How could some people remember the entire periodic table? But they could. There were these special guys—different from the rest of us—mental prodigies.

At college, these brainiacs were called nerds, and despised, but not by him, even though he was captain of the basketball team and was supposed to despise them. He didn't say so at the time (he was a politician even back then), but he thought they were awesome.

On top of this, he had always been impressed by the English accent. It sounded so cultured, so refined. For President Dale, Professor Donald Kessler, a brainiac with an English accent, was a slam-dunk.

"The Martian canals are actually canyons," Kessler was saying. "Some of them are over a hundred miles deep. I think we can assume that Martian civilization has developed *under the surface* of the planet."

The First Lady didn't like this Martian civilization. She didn't like that it had developed under the surface of the planet. It seemed suspiciously furtive. And why were they choosing now to come out into the open? Suddenly, there was a whole Martian civilization to contend with that hadn't been there yesterday. It was disturbing and she didn't like it. Her female intuition told her: beware!

Rusty, the dog, didn't understand what was going on. But he loved being there on the couch with his owners. His eyes shone and his tongue lolled and he enjoyed the fantasy that he was human.

In another part of Washington, Louise Williams, back from work, was relaxing in front of the TV. She, too, was watching Donald Kessler.

"Their science and technology must be absolutely mind-boggling," he said. "They'll have an awful lot to teach us."

Louise heard a door bang. She turned. Cedric and Neville were shambling across the living room, their baggy pants flapping, their fancy print boxer shorts sticking, jailhouse-style, out the back.

"Where you going? I want to talk to you."

Her two rebel sons pretended not to hear, and loped purposefully to the front door.

"Hey! Come back here!"

Cedric and Neville slammed out.

On TV, Nathalie frowned.

"But why haven't we seen any evidence of Martians before, Professor?"

"I believe we have," Donald replied coolly.

"You mean, UFOs?"

"Yes, exactly."

In New York, in his office at the General News Networks building, Jason Stone and two other reporters, watched the same TV interview. Jason watched with a faintly sickened expression—*he* should have been doing this interview.

"I see, so, what in your opinion are some of the things the Martians can teach us?" asked Nathalie of the famous professor.

Donald leaned toward her, twinkling. "Quite a lot about Mars I expect!" Nathalie laughed.

Watching, Jason shook his head. "You see that? He's flirting with her! You see that?"

The other reporters shrugged. "So what?"

In the TV studio, the cameras moved silently around the small set like sharks around a pair of seals. The heat of the halogen lights and the proximity of Nathalie was having an effect on Donald Kessler. He was loosening up. He even felt a little intoxicated.

"But, really, this is tremendously exciting,"

he said. "We're on the brink of a Copernican change—a new renaissance! Think of it! The knowledge, the new ideas! It's going to change the world! It's going to change everything! We must be open! Embrace it! Don't you realize, Nathalie? We are being given a very, very big present."

"You mean like Christmas?" Nathalie's eyes were wide.

Kessler nodded.

"Exactly like Christmas, only, instead of toys and games and Christmas crackers and paper hats, we'll be opening presents with knowledge in them!"

Nathalie felt like she was fifteen years old again and in class with Mr. Baxter.

"Who knows what they know?" said Kessler. "Maybe they have traveled beyond our solar system? Maybe they possess propulsion devices that go faster than light? Maybe they can tell us about the Universe—how it started, where it's going, perhaps even its purpose! It's tremendously exciting, Nathalie! This is the most important thing to have happened since . . . oh, since Newton discovered gravity!"

Abruptly, without warning, the TV monitors, which were all showing the talking heads of Donald and Nathalie, began fluorescing. In the control booth, the director was alarmed.

"What's happening, Liam? What's wrong with the picture?"

"I don't know," said Liam, bewildered.

"Go to camera two!" yelled the director.

The assistant mixer was pounding a button on the control desk. "I can't, it's busted!"

"Then go to one! Go to four!"

On all the monitors the picture was distorting. The mixing desk phone rang and Liam grabbed it. He listened for a moment and turned pale.

"What is it?" said the director.

"It's Engineering," said Liam. "Something is jamming our signal!"

The TV technicians looked helplessly at the monitors. The image had almost completely dissolved and a new image was beginning to form.

Over at GNN, Jason was trying to fix the television. "Maybe it's the cable?" said one of the reporters.

Jason examined the back of the TV but everything looked normal. The TV screen seemed to be showing an out-of-focus Bigfoot fighting through a heavy snowstorm. Jason banged the set with his fist. The picture cleared.

"Jesus, what's that?" said the reporter from the sports desk.

Jason peered around. What he saw on the screen was the face of something from a nightmare. The face had no flesh. There were teeth, a bony jaw, a vestigial bone-nose, and an enormous, skull-less brain. The exposed brain was covered in a ganglion of pulsating blood vessels, and, below the bony forehead, were two bulging red eyes. The demon had a neck, shoulders, and arms—and five fingers on each hand. You couldn't see much of its body because it was wrapped in a large iridescent magenta cloak with a weirdly curlicued collar.

"Is this some kind of a joke?" demanded Jason.

Two thousand miles west, in Las Vegas, Byron Williams and Cindy, the cocktail waitress, were standing in the Isis Sports Bar—aghast. Surrounded by tourists from Salt Lake City, they stared at the TV showing the skull-face with the red eyes and the giant brain. A female voice broke through above the TV static.

"This is Nathalie West," it said. "You can't see me because the picture signal is being jammed. The station engineers have told us the source of the signal is beyond our planet. So we believe that what you're seeing . . . is probably a Martian!"

Cindy felt a chill snake through her like she'd just stepped on freezing cold tiles. Man, was it ugly!

"That's a Martian?" Byron said, echoing everyone's thoughts.

In Washington, D.C., in the White House, in her bedroom, on her bed, Taffy was lying on her stomach, eating Chee•tos. She gaped at the TV. "That's a Martian?" she said out loud.

In Perkinsville, Kansas, at the back of the donut shop, Richie's joint had gone out but he didn't notice. He was gawking at the Martian on TV.

Maria, the depressed Mexican counter-wiper, stood behind him, her eyes narrowed, her lip curled down in a sneer.

"Whoa, Maria!" said Richie. "Lookit the size of that brain! He must be really smart!"

In the White House, in their private living room, the President and the First Lady stared at the TV.

"Yikes!" said the President.

"Oh my God!" said the First Lady.

Rusty, their golden retriever, dropped his head and emitted a low growl.

Then the Martian began to speak. If his appearance was scary, his voice was worse. It sounded like a mix between a rattlesnake and a screeching crow. His harsh, hissing, grating squawks gave an instant headache. The First

Lady's chin was buried in her neck, her eyes wide with alarm, and her hands were gripping the pearls around her neck.

"I am *not* having that thing in my house!" she said.

The President had the queasy feeling he experienced when he had to do a U-turn on a campaign promise.

"We might have to, Marsha. People are going to expect us to meet with them."

Marsha Dale's lips tightened. "Well," she announced rigidly, "they are *not* eating off the Van Buren china!"

In the TV studio, there was an eerie stillness. The director, technicians, and crew people watched the studio monitors. The grotesque, gesticulating Martian made Nathalie feel sick. She held Donald Kessler's right arm tightly with both hands.

"Ugh . . . it's *gross*!" she whispered.

Kessler looked at the squawking Martian with detached, scientific interest.

"Don't forget, Nathalie, that we will look equally 'gross' to him."

Nathalie gazed up at Donald. This man made her feel safe. Her mind opened to him. She understood.

"Oh yeah, like the blond niece on *The Munsters*."

Kessler frowned. What was she talking about?

In Perkinsville, Kansas, at the back of the donut shop, Richie and Maria were transfixed by the talking ghoul. The Martian's bony fingers gesticulated. Then he stopped screeching, made a low bow, and, straightening up, slowly drew a large circle in the air.

"Whoa!" cried Richie. "He just made the international sign of the donut!" The TV screen flashed and the Martian was gone.

In Las Vegas, in the Isis Sports Bar, the crowd watching the TV screens stood in stunned silence. Suddenly, *Today In Fashion with Nathalie West* was back on air. Unaware they were being watched, Nathalie and Kessler were clutching each other.

In Jason's office, the reporters all talked at once. Jason was outraged at the sight of his girlfriend being so intimate with the professor. "Lookit that! Look what he's doing! You see that! He just copped a feel!" Jason turned to his colleagues for support, but they were all talking excitedly about the Martian.

Chapter 10

From the Halls of Montezuma,
To the shores of Tripoli;
We fight our country's battles
In the air, on land, and sea;
First to fight for right and freedom
And to keep our honor clean;
We are proud to claim the title of
United States Marine.

If the Founding Fathers could return to America in the beginning years of the twenty-first century to inspect the political system they had created in the closing years of the eighteenth century, they would find much to surprise them.

The writers of the Constitution would surely catch their breath at the sheer size of the federal bureaucracy. They would marvel at the power of the judiciary, the importance of political parties, the immense magnitude of the defense establishment, and the loss of power suffered by the individual states.

No changes would be more astounding than those surrounding the Presidency. The founders had assumed that the legislative branch of the government, and especially the House of Representatives, would reflect and enact the will of the people. The President was expected to administer the laws that Congress passed.

But today these roles have, somehow, become reversed. Congress seems largely reduced to tinkering with presidential suggestions. And the House of Representatives is less the guardian of the democratic spirit than it is the home of special interests.

Today, most Americans believe it is the President who embodies the popular will, who provides the energy behind public policy, and who suggests and markets new laws. Over the past two centuries, power has become more and more concentrated in the office of the President.

James Dale thought it was too much for one guy. He had to deal with every goddamn problem. Yesterday it was the Cubans, now it was the Martians. He'd had only three hours' sleep the night before, a lousy breakfast, no lunch, had performed a mighty speech to the nation, and now he was in the National Defense building, conferring on strategy with a bunch of strange-smelling military chiefs.

He was seated at the conference table with his

old campaign buddy, Howard Runyon—now secretary of defense, the four Joint Chiefs, General Jack Decker, General Bill Casey, Jerry Ross, and a German linguist named Dr. Herman Ziegler.

At one side of the room stood three easels holding charts. On the first chart was a poorly executed drawing of a Martian with a horizontal graph line next to it marking off the centimeters. This showed the Martian to be 108 centimeters high—what is that in feet and inches? The second chart was festooned with photos of the Martian fleet, which Dale had seen before. The third chart was a drawing of Mars and Earth with connecting lines and vectors. What was that for?

Standing before the charts, pipe in mouth, pointer in hand, stood the debonair Professor Kessler. "From the limited information available, I've made three extrapolations," he said. "One: Our Martian friend is a carbon-based lifeform. Two: he breathes nitrogen. And three: the large cerebrum, here"—he pointed with his pointer—"indicates telepathic potential."

Jerry Ross didn't like the idea that the Martians were telepathic—that would cause all kinds of trouble. He put up his hand. He wanted clarification. "Does this mean they can read our thoughts?" he asked.

"Potentially, yes," said Kessler.

General Decker scowled. This Brit nancy boy gave him a pain. Why were they listening to this fruitbar? They should be marshaling the troops! Readying their weapons systems! Maybe even trying a preemptive strike?

Decker remembered the time his commanding officer conducted a strategy meeting, during the "Vietnam Conflict," and they were hit by a bombing raid. The North Vietnamese didn't fanny around having meetings—they got out there and kicked ass! Decker glanced at the Joint Chiefs. They were looking stern—their posture of choice when in doubt.

The President leaned forward. "How about their intentions, Professor? Are they friendly?"

Kessler nodded slowly. "Given their extremely high level of technical development, logic dictates they are an advanced culture. Therefore they are more than likely to be peaceful and enlightened. On the other hand, the human race is, I fear, an underdeveloped and dangerously aggressive species."

He peered meaningfully over his spectacles. "It's my belief they will have more to fear from us than we from them."

General Decker was disgusted. He didn't need speculation—he needed facts! He glanced at the military chiefs, to see how they were taking it. As usual, they looked stern.

Kessler turned to Dr. Ziegler. "Doctor, would you care to take the floor?"

"Thank you, Professor."

Dr. Ziegler got up and walked over to the main-frame computer beside the charts.

Kessler sat down next to General Casey as the German doctor adjusted levels on his billion-operations-per-second computer.

"So," said Dr. Ziegler, "for many years I have been refining a translating computer." Ziegler spoke with a heavy German accent.

"I haff broken down two hundred and tventy-seven phonemes, forty-eight diphthongs, and two hundred and ninety-two other sounds in a four-point five-octave range."

Dr. Ziegler flicked a switch and the video terminal blinked on. "I haff run ze Martian transmission through seven different linguistics programs. The resultz are not perfect. But zis may answer some of your questions."

He pressed a button and the coarse voice of the Martian ambassador was heard. Then, he adjusted some controls. Tapes revolved, and the computer's synthesized voice spoke: ". . . All green of skin, eight hundred centuries ago. Their bodily fluids include the birth of half-breeds."

The President took notes. He leaned across to Jerry. "How many centuries ago?"

General Casey jumped in. "Eight hundred, Mr. President."

The synthesized voice continued: "For the fundamental truth is self-determination of the cosmos, for dark is the suede that mows like a harvest."

"What the hell is that supposed to mean?" complained General Decker. All around the conference table, no one spoke. Kessler sucked on his pipe. Dr. Ziegler scratched his head. They were all flummoxed.

Meanwhile, across Pennsylvania Avenue, in the White House, the melancholy Taffy made her way down the West corridor. She was holding a drawing pad and colored pencils, intending to go to the Lincoln Room to sketch the Bellini statue of Orpheus.

A Secret Service man was standing at the end of the hallway. He put his arm out, preventing her from passing. "You can't come this way. There's a tour in progress," he said, from behind his dark glasses.

Taffy looked at his deadpan face. What went on in that brain? It seemed as if the human race produced a special species of meathead specifically designed for stopping you getting into places—clubs, bars, parties, military installations, rooms . . . She actually knew this guy—his name was Clark. But it made no difference. Orders were orders. Tours had priority. Taffy didn't have the energy to argue or flirt. It just confirmed her belief that life was a party she hadn't been invited to.

She retraced her steps. Maybe she should go out and sketch in the Rose Garden? But then she remembered her mother was using it for a "Daughters of the Revolution" buffet and fundraiser.

She felt a stab of loneliness. She wanted to call somebody, to get out of this wedding-cake hell—to escape. Okay, so she was only fifteen, but she felt fully grown-up now. Nobody realized that! They all treated her like a child!

What was the point of anything? What was the point of trying to be a good artist? How many daughters of the President of the United States had become good painters? None. Picasso's father was a mule-skinner, wasn't he?

She was doomed by her birth. The only thing she could hope to be was an ex-alcoholic with a book deal to write about what monsters her parents were. And she had to wait twenty years before she could even do that! What she needed was a boyfriend, a boyfriend with piercings and tattoos and a bad attitude.

Way across the country, in the fabled city of Las Vegas, in a church hall between the Strip and Downtown, an AA meeting was in progress. Forty-three recovering alcoholics, all smoking cigarettes, were sitting in folding chairs watching Barbara Land, who had just gotten on stage.

"Hello, my name is Barbara."

"Hello, Barbara!!!"

Barbara felt thrilled to be up there in front of others who had suffered. By respecting them, she was respecting herself. By accepting and forgiving them, and applauding their efforts to remain sober, she was accepting, forgiving, and applauding herself. She took a deep breath.

"I'm an alcoholic—but I haven't had a drink in three months."

Everyone clapped. The applause washed over her like sparkling foam.

"Thank you! Thank you!" cried Barbara, smiling. "And I'm feeling so optimistic because of these Martians. We're not alone in the Universe! And it's so perfect that it's happening at the beginning of the new millennium!"

The eyes of the ex-boozers were shining upon her—earnest and full of support.

"Our planet was suffering, with the ozone and the rain forest, and so many people unhappy in their lives. But then the Martians heard our global cry for help. People say they're ugly, but I think they're here to show us the way! They've come to save us!"

The crowd cheered and applauded. Barbara smiled tearfully, put her palms together in a Buddhist blessing, and recited: "Nam As Dei! Nam As Dei! Nam As Dei!"

In Perkinsville, Kansas, the Norris family came out of their trailer. The Greyhound to the army base was due in ten minutes.

Billy-Glenn, looking spiffy in the uniform of an army private, first class, was holding hands with his girlfriend, Meg, a cutie who worked at Ace Video Rentals. Richie and his mother, Sue-Ann, helped Grandma into her wheelchair, and they all headed over to the bus stop.

As they moseyed through the trailer park and down the dirt road to the highway, Glenn Norris regaled his family with his thoughts about America. "The way I see it, is that America is just the greatest little country that there is. Whatever you want, America has it, right here! A fine, freedom-loving country, democracy, free speech, freedom of religion, everything. And you know what the greatest freedom of all is? Well, let me tell you: it's freedom of opportunity. A man wants to improve himself, make his way in the world by his hard work and his efforts, he can do that. If he works hard and lives a decent kind of a life, there's no limit to where he can get to, right up to one day becoming the President of the United States if that's what he's got a mind to. I'm a patriotic American. That's not too fashionable a thing to say these days, but that's what I am. "My country, right or wrong," straight down the line. And I think those that don't see it like that can't call themselves real Americans and they shouldn't be allowed to. If they're not prepared to die for their country when the call comes, well then, they shouldn't be allowed to partake in the benefits of their country that other people have fought and died for so they could have them. You hear these people on the TV and in the newspapers and they're saying things like that America is not doing right here or what other foreign countries are saying that's criticizing America—and those people, they're being paid thousands of dollars for saying unpatriotic things about the country. How crazy can you get? They're communists, those people, they're people dedicated to destroying the American way of life—and they're getting paid by the lefties who run our news media to do it! And what does the great American public do? It sits there and lets them get away with it! Any other country in the world, they'd take them out and shoot them! Like I say, America's the greatest country the world's ever seen, and if a person don't think so, then why don't they go live someplace else?''

"You said it, Dad!" declared Billy-Glenn, putting his duffel bag on the ground. They had reached the bus stop.

Billy-Glenn's girlfriend, Meg, was not saying much. She loved Billy-Glenn even though she didn't really know him. But when has love cared about knowing someone?

The bus appeared around the corner and Meg threw her arms around her soldier boyfriend and started to cry. Sue-Ann pushed her big gut in between them, grabbed his head, and kissed him on the cheek.

"Bye bye, honey, bye bye."

"Be careful, baby," said Meg, her mascara running down her cheeks in rivulets. "Don't get killed or anything."

"Aww, ain't she cute?" said Billy-Glenn.

His father clapped him on the back. "We're real proud of you, son."

"Thanks, Dad."

Richie shook his brother's hand. "So long, bro."

"So long, retard, just don't touch any of my stuff while I'm gone."

Infected by the sweet pain of leave-taking, Grandma burst into tears. Her skinny fingers reached out, trembling. "Good-bye, Thomas."

"It's Billy-Glenn, Grandma," said Billy-Glenn.

Sue-Ann wiped her eyes. "Now, you take good care, you hear?"

"I will, Mama."

The bus door was open and the driver was waiting. Billy-Glenn kissed his sweetheart, Meg, on the mouth. She clung to him. She didn't want to let go, but he unhooked her hands from his neck. "I gotta proceed, Meg."

He picked up his duffel bag and turned to the others. "Adios!"

"Bye! Bye now! Bye!"

Everybody waved as he climbed aboard the bus. The door closed, and it drove away in a cloud of dust.

The Norris family tramped back home. Nobody spoke. Richie felt the silence willing him to fill it.

"Well, he's gone for a while," he said unimaginatively.

Meg glanced at him, through tear-streaked eyes. His mother gave him a moist, disapproving look.

"Oh, Richie, why can't you be more like your brother?"

"We was lucky with Billy-Glenn," pronounced the dad. "You can't expect the same luck twice."

Richie stared at the ground. He'd had this all his life.

"Hey, Richie," said Glenn. "You wanna do something useful?"

"Yeah, sure, Dad."

"Okay, you can take Grandma back to the home."

Twenty minutes later, Grandma was seat-belted into the passenger seat of the Norris's red Ford pickup and Richie was driving her the six miles to the Nightingale Retirement Home. This was where Grandma lived when she wasn't visiting at the trailer.

Richie loved his Grandma. When he was a kid, she had been unfailingly kind to him. Richie was more sensitive than the rest of his family, and he responded well to kindness. It was from his Grandma that he'd learned to love music. She had introduced him to the greatest composers of her day, such men as Hank Williams, Slim Whitman, Eddie Burns, Sylvester Cotton, and Big Bill Broonzy.

"Say, Grandma." Richie turned the wheel. "I bet you never thought you'd live to see Martians coming to Earth. Pretty far-out, huh?"

She stared out through the windshield, a trail of drool dribbling slowly down her chin.

"But then just think of all the crazy stuff

you've seen in your lifetime! I bet people were scared when they invented the train."

"Boy, I ain't that old!" said Grandma.

Richie had to stop himself from instinctively braking. You could talk to Grandma all day and not get a single rational response, but then, when you least expected it, she'd come out with something. It was weird. Most of the time she was as remote as a concrete brick.

Grandma fell forward, banged her head on the dash, and jerked right back up again.

"You okay?" Richie hoped he could get her to the Nightingale without any mishaps. The nerve-racking thing about Grandma was that she could die at any time. He knew if she deceased in the truck while he was driving, he'd be blamed forevermore. Besides, he didn't want her to decease. Even though she was only sporadically present, she was his Grandma—and when she was gone, his world would feel empty.

The back of her head was on the car seat and she was staring up at the roof, a dazed expression on her face. But there was no cut on her forehead.

"Are you sure you're okay?"

"I want to get back to Slim," Grandma said in a hoarse whisper. "Slim and Muffy and Richie."

"I'm Richie," said Richie.

"I know. Richie was the best one."

Richie sighed and concentrated on driving. It was no use trying to talk to her.

He studied the road ahead. They were passing through a grove of eucalyptus trees. Richie wondered who had planted them. Eucalyptus trees came from Australia. Maybe a hundred years ago, some homesick Australian had planted them. They sure looked wrong here on the flat Kansas plain, but they were welcome. The only things taller were the electricity pylon towers that strode across the flatland from one horizon to the other, and were the tallest structures in the state of Kansas except for the Topeka Radio Tower.

Fifteen minutes later, the dusty red pickup reached the entrance to the Nightingale Retirement Home. It was a large, low, one-story building with seventy-five rooms, purpose-built in the 1950s as a nursing home.

Richie got out, went around, and lifted the folded-up wheelchair out of the back. He stretched it out, kicked down the locking bar, then wheeled it to the passenger side and opened the door.

"Okay, you ready for this?"

He slid one arm under Grandma's legs, the other arm around her back, and lifted her out. She was such a frail old thing, no more than ninety pounds, and her skin was like rice paper. He gently lowered her into the wheelchair. Grandma didn't say a word.

Richie pushed her through the entrance into the lobby where a few old people were sitting in armchairs watching the *Lawrence Welk Show* on TV.

A formidable middle-aged Asian nurse, named Mrs. Dong, came up the corridor. "Hello, Richie," she called. "Are you bringing Mrs. Norris back?"

"Yes, shall I wheel her through?"

"Yes, I come with you. They cleaned her room—it's probably locked."

Richie, Grandma, and Mrs. Dong went down the corridor, all the way to the end, passing door after identical door.

Grandma had one of the better rooms, with two windows, and a view of the flower garden at the back, although the garden had recently been destroyed by Mr. Harris, a ninety-year-old ex-bank president, who had gone berserk, believing he was back at Guadalcanal in WW II.

Mrs. Dong unlocked Grandma's door.

"Thanks," said Richie, and wheeled her in.

Grandma's room was cluttered with her memories. The bed, in an alcove, was surrounded by framed photographs on the walls and on the bedside table.

Richie lifted her out of the wheelchair and put her down into her favorite old rocker. Next to the rocking chair was the most important thing she possessed: her "Celebrity" sound system. A cabinet stood next to it, on which was displayed her collection of glass animals and her favorite cat, Muffy, now stuffed.

Richie looked around the room. Even though it had just been cleaned, it still smelled of old drapes.

"Are you gonna be all right?"

Grandma wasn't listening. She was leaning over the turntable. With shaking hands, she turned it on and dropped the needle on to the disc.

"If you need anything—any donuts or anything—call me, okay?"

The speakers suddenly blasted out the music of Slim Whitman singing, "I'm Casting My Lasso Towards The Sky."

Grandma closed her eyes and smiled blissfully. A moment later, Mrs. Dong stormed into the room. "Too loud! Too loud! Turn music down!"

"Okay," said Richie. "I know how to handle this. Wait just one second." Richie picked up the headphones and plugged them in. The music stopped. Grandma opened her eyes and looked stricken. Richie positioned the headphones over her ears. She sighed with relief.

"All right now?"

"You show her how use headphones," ordered Mrs. Dong.

"Okay, I will. I've been trying, but it takes her awhile."

Mrs. Dong shook her finger threateningly. "Use headphones, or no music!" She left the room.

Chapter 11

"Men use thought to justify their injustices, and speech to conceal their thoughts."

—Voltaire

Was Arthur Land an ambitious man? Does Howdy Doody have wooden balls? Art was so extravagantly egotistical that his wife, Barbara, had once tried to encourage him to lower his self-esteem.

"It's good for you," she'd told him. "Repeat after me: 'I'm no better than the poor slobs sleeping on bus benches.' "

But it had no effect.

Born in Reno, Nevada, Art's father was a two-bit lawyer who seldom got a case and spent most of his time exercising his elbows in bars. His mother had had many suitors—she had the love letters to prove it—but she had turned them all down for his dad.

Why did she marry such a loser? His dad had been good-looking, in a long-necked Oklahoma farm-boy kind of way, maybe that was the reason? Anyhow, all she did throughout his childhood was complain she'd married the wrong guy.

Art was the eldest son, the apple of his mother's angry eye. She was determined he would succeed where her husband had failed. Arthur would bring glory to the family name.

He began his first business enterprise when he was nine. It was his own idea. Christmas trees. He planted Christmas trees in the backyard. The seeds cost five cents apiece. He planted one hundred of them. All he had to do was water them, and in three years' time, at Christmas, sell them for ten dollars each. This represented a clear profit of ten thousand percent! Unfortunately, as soon as the shoots came up, they were eaten by rabbits. His next business scheme fared no better. He saved up a whole year's money from his paper-route earnings to purchase a badge-making machine.

There was an election coming up and the candidates and their supporters needed badges. But when he tried to execute his first order, the machine broke, and, by the time the new parts had arrived from Germany, the election was over.

When he was fifteen he got a break. His

friend, Dave, showed him how to cheat at poker. He could still remember the exultation— walking away from the table, pockets stuffed with green, knowing he'd suckered the yo-yo's who'd trusted him. He couldn't help it if people were stupid.

One of the most stupid characteristics of people is they like to gamble. Gambling is dumb. The only way you can win is either by cheating or by owning the gambling operation.

At the age of seventeen, he went into a business partnership with Dave's father, who ran a small numbers racket for some mob bosses in Omaha, Nebraska. Dave's father was always spouting mottos like: "Winning isn't everything, but it sure beats losing," or "Crime doesn't pay unless you can afford a good lawyer." He was a cute guy.

He introduced Art to the mob bosses, who liked him because he looked so all-American. Art was a fresh-faced young man with thick, blond hair and an easy grin. He reminded people of the young Jimmy Stewart.

Dave's dad, and his shadowy supervisors, had long wanted to set up a bingo business in Reno, but they couldn't get a state license. However, with the young, innocent-looking Art as their frontman, they were successful. Not only did Art charm the state gambling board into granting him a license, but they also gave him a special low-interest government loan. Of course there were conditions to the loan, but it was like trying to leash a dog with sausages. In ten years, Art became the majority owner of twenty-four highly successful bingo halls.

Those were the good old days. But the new days looked pretty good, too! Art leaned back in his personally designed reclining office chair, which was covered in black-and-white calfskin, and blew a perfect smoke ring from his Monte Cristo cigar.

The intercom buzzed. Art pressed a button. "What's up, honey pie?"

"It's your wife on line one," said the smooth voice of Melanie, his secretary.

"I'm not here. Did you get that address for Byron?"

The secretary gave him Byron's address, which he wrote down on his Hermés pad. Suddenly he had an idea about how to do the restaurants.

"Hey, Melanie, you know how we've been busting our buns trying to come up with themes for the restaurants?"

"Yes."

"Well how about this: Martian-style."

"Martian-style?"

"Yes, you know, we find out how the Martians do their restaurants and we copy it! It's great! We'll be the first guys in Vegas to do the Martian thing! But, hey, listen: Don't tell anyone, okay?"

"Okay, Mr. Land."

"Good. Now, we need pictures. Martian stuff. Anything you can get. See what you can rustle up, okay?"

"Yes, sir."

He clicked off the intercom, leaned back in his chair, put his hands behind his head, and rested one of his cowboy-booted feet up on the bird's-eye maple desk. "Hmm," he mused. "The Martian Lounge . . . The Red Planet Pizza Kitchen . . . Mars-burgers!"

Back in Washington, D.C., in the White House Press Room, Jerry Ross faced a noisy crowd of reporters. Everyone was claiming his attention. Jerry felt like a zookeeper at the penguin enclosure with a bucket full of fish.

"Wait, wait, wait a second—we'll get to questions later. Right now, all I can tell you is the President is talking to other world leaders and they're preparing a shopping list of issues of common interest to discuss. There's a concerted, unilateral diplomatic effort being made."

The journalists were all shouting and waving their arms.

"Jerry! Jerry! Jerry!"

Jerry sighed and pointed to a man he recognized in the front row.

"Yes? You."

The other journalists quieted down. Jason Stone had the floor.

"Mr. Ross, if the Martians land, will the press have access? Can we do interviews?"

Jerry had no idea what the hell would happen. He'd have to bluff his way through questions, keeping his dignity, and making it look like he was in control.

"That depends," said Jerry. "We need to establish contact, work out whatever communication problems, and set the parameters for talks."

Jason and the other journalists looked peeved. They knew when they were being hornswoggled.

"Then, I guess we'll just have to see how things develop. Next?" Jerry pointed to a journalist in a silk tie and an Armani suit.

"Do the Martians use money like we do?"

"Money? I don't exactly know . . ." He felt something behind him and glanced around. James Dale was coming through the drapes. Jerry felt relieved; now the President could take over.

"Ladies and gentlemen," he said. "Thanks for your patience . . . here's the President."

Jerry stepped down and Dale came on to the podium. "Good morning," he said, looking around and smiling.

"Nice to see you all again. I only have a few minutes for questions, so let's get started . . ."

Everyone put up their hands.

The President pointed to an asexual-looking woman in a dark, nondescript suit. "Yes? Do you have a question?"

"Do the Martians have two sexes like we do?"

James Dale hated these press conferences. He always had to be courteous and good-humored. If he evinced anything even faintly uncivil, it would be blown up into some monstrously negative story in the next day's news. He smiled and nodded to the asexual journalist.

"That's a very interesting question, uh, sir, ma'am . . . I'm glad you asked me that. As a matter of fact, as far as we can tell right now, the Martians are bipedal, carbon-based life-forms who are, clearly, of extremely high intelligence, but, as far as their sexual characteristics are concerned, it would be unwise and maybe even counterproductive to speculate at this time. Next?"

The journalists all had their hands up.

"Mr. President! Mr. President! Mr. President!"

It was 6:30 P.M. Pacific Coast Time and Byron Williams sat alone in his kitchen. In front of him lay his scrapbook of press clippings. He had just finished a "solo meal" courtesy of Chef Boy-ardie, and was sipping from a forty-ouncer of malt liquor. He felt like shit.

What is it about human nature? Why, when we feel bad, do we seek solace in making ourselves feel even worse? Byron knew a surefire way to go from mere unhappiness to total misery—to get out his scrapbook.

Slowly, he turned the pages. Here, in newspaper clippings and magazine tearoffs, was a chronicle of his days of glory. There was a picture of him with Joe Frazier, another with Sonny Liston, and here he was goofing off with Muhammed Ali.

It all seemed so long ago. He couldn't believe he was the same man portrayed in these photographs—so young, handsome, and beautifully fit.

Byron had reigned for two and a half years. He was unbeatable then and lived the life of a god. But the terrible thing was he *couldn't even remember it*. If it weren't for these press clippings, he'd have no proof it had ever happened.

Chugging on the forty-ouncer, he leafed through to the end. On the last page was a small, Scotch-taped clipping that dated from five years after his defeat by Ali and his subsequent downward slide. The small headline stated: EX-CHAMP ARRESTED FOR SPOUSAL ABUSE. He glanced at the inset picture of Louise, positioned in the corner of a larger photograph of himself in handcuffs, being thrust into the back of a squad car.

He closed the book and sighed. Maybe now would be the right time to commit suicide? But no, he was too damned miserable to kill himself. He would do it when he was happy. He wanted to go out on a high.

But what could get him high? Drugs? No, he'd tried them all and the states they put you in were artificial. Booze? Booze made the pain stop but there was no real happiness in it. There was only one thing that could make him feel good: to have Louise love him again. And were that ever to happen, he would no longer want to kill himself. That's what you call a conundrum. Life was full of 'em. Byron closed the book and decided to go jogging.

Below the distant mountains that contained the man-made miracle of Hoover Dam, the sun was setting. The city of Las Vegas was beginning to don its party clothes, and Byron Williams, the hood of his sweatshirt low over his face, jogged down Sixth Street.

A dark stretch limousine glided around the corner. Byron glanced back. Was it his imagination, or was the car tailing him? Wary, but un-afraid, Byron began jogging in place. If something was going to go down, he wanted to get right to it.

The limo pulled up alongside him and the tinted passenger window hissed open. Art Land's genial face looked out.

"Good evening, Byron. I see you're carless. You want a ride?"

"No, can't you see I'm jogging?"

Art opened the limo door. "Get in. I got a proposition for you."

Byron raised an eyebrow. He had a bad feeling about this. "What kind of proposition?"

"Get in and I'll tell ya."

"Not interested."

"Byron! I've got a real proposition for you. You're gonna like it, I'm serious."

Byron jogged away.

"Don't you want to make some money? I'm offering you money here!"

Money. Byron needed money. Maybe he should find out what Mr. Creepy had to say?

Later, Art and Byron sat in the back of the moving limo. Art was drinking Glenlivet, Byron was drinking lemonade. The chauffeur was unseen behind a dark glass partition.

"Byron, I want to do you a favor. I owe you. I

made a lot of money off your fight in Jamaica in seventy-three."

"I'm glad somebody did," said Byron.

Art swirled the ice in his glass.

"I know it's tough for athletes. You hit a certain age, opportunities dry up. So, here's the deal."

He paused, building up the suspense.

"There's this skunk owes me money. He needs a wake-up call. I want you to go visit with him and use that famous left hook. What do you say? How about it?"

Without moving, Byron said: "I used to fight in the ring, Art—the ring."

"I know that, but this is a professional assignment. I'll pay you two grand." Art gave him his best ingenuous look.

"That's fair, isn't it? Listen, as soon as it's done, come to my office. I'll give you cash."

Byron looked at the floor, gripping his glass in both hands. He gave Art a furtive glance. Art reminded him of an evil Jimmy Stewart.

"This ain't funny," he said. "I'm trying to get back with my wife! We had a problem with this before, but I changed myself."

Byron was gripping his glass so tightly, Art was worried he'd break it. Byron growled in his face. "I found Allah. I gave up pork and I'm a better man. I tamed that bull . . . *and I don't want to bring him out!*"

"Okay, okay, you gave up pork—I get it." Art was scared. "It was just an idea, that's all. Where can I drop you?"

Chapter 12

Now it is the time of night
  That the graves, all gaping wide,
Every one lets forth his sprite,
  In the church-way paths to glide.

—William Shakespeare,
A Midsummer Night's Dream.

It was the dead of night. In a hidden desert valley, in New Mexico, in the upper laboratory of a radio telescope, four eager men were gathered around a screen. They were the night staff of a classified military tracking station known only as "Base 47."

The screen was filled with racing numbers. The base captain looked at the NASA tech who'd been drafted in to handle extraterrestrial communications.

"What does it mean?"

The NASA tech grinned. He was excited.

"It's the Martians! They're sending *coordinates*!"

At 3:58 A.M. on Saturday, May 13, 2003, in the President's private living room in the White House, a bleary Dale, wearing only his bathrobe, was slumped at his desk. Facing him were Professor Donald Kessler, General Jack Decker, and General Bill Casey. Outside, the city of Washington was abed and all was quiet. Political crises are like newborn babies—they get you up in the middle of the night.

"Where are they landing?" said the President.

"Pahrump," said Professor Kessler. "It's in the Nevada Desert."

General Decker stepped forward. "Mr. President, my reserve troops are on full alert. They can be there at 0:800 hours."

Professor Donald Kessler butted in. "Sir, we must not send the wrong message to these people! We need a welcome mat, not a row of tanks!"

Decker snorted like a derisive wart hog. "Hey, you want Martians roaming across Nevada without security?"

"You're right, General," said Dale, his voice slurring with fatigue, like a misstepped skater sliding across the ice. "This needs to be supervised."

His first instinct was to be there to greet the Martians, but Decker's mention of security gave him pause. There was always a chance they could be hostile, despite what everyone was saying. Anyway, it would lessen his authority if he was there.

Dale knew from history the importance of ambassadors in allaying anxiety and preparing the ground. What he needed was to pick an ambassador. Who? He looked at Decker. No, not him—too volatile. He looked at General Casey. Casey was asleep on the Chesterfield.

"General Casey?"

Casey's eyes sprang open. "Yessir!"

"Do you think you can handle this?"

"Yessir!"

Decker ground his teeth. The man didn't even know what they were talking about!

"But, Bill, keep a lid on it, huh?" confided the President.

"Keep a lid on it, yessir."

"A few key media, a cross-section of invited guests—we'll have to tell a few foreign governments—but we don't want this to be a zoo, is that clear?"

"Yessir," said Casey.

Kessler wrinkled his nose. Maybe Casey hadn't been asleep, after all?

"So, when do you want me to start?" asked Casey.

This threw the President for a moment. "Well, I guess you could start right now."

"Yessir."

Casey got up and straightened his three-star-general uniform.

"So, what are we doing exactly?"

Sometime later, General Decker stormed down the third-floor corridor, fuming. He could not believe the President's ignorance of military protocol! An important assignment like Martian security should *not* be put in the hands of a three-star general when a four-star general, such as he, was available! It was unconscionable! He was so angry there was only one thing he could do: go home and do three complete reps of the Canadian Air Force exercises.

As he marched down the corridor, he shouted out loud: "This country's in the hands of half-wits! It's an outrage!"

A door opened and Taffy looked out. She was in her nightgown, rubbing her eyes sleepily.

"Hey, you want to keep it down? People live here!"

Decker looked at her, startled.

She slammed the door.

Chapter 13

Gather ye rosebuds while ye may,
  Old Time is still a-flying;
And this same flower that smiles today
  Tomorrow will be dying.

—Robert Herrick

The previous night, Jason and Nathalie had gone to Raoul's and had a romantic dinner. After the first bottle of Bordeaux, he'd forgiven her for getting the Kessler interview—and by the end of the second bottle, he was begging her to come home with him. She lived in SoHo, just three blocks away, but he didn't like staying over at her place—she always had so many phone messages. He could only enjoy being with her if he was in control. And now, since her Kessler scoop, he especially needed her to submit to him. The trace of resentment he felt acted like an aphrodisiac.

Nathalie knew he was embittered, and, if she went back with him, their lovemaking would be rough. But she kind of felt in the mood for that this evening. But she didn't want him to get *too* confident, so she insisted they go back to her place first and pick up the dog. Jason hated Poppy, so this was a small personal victory.

The early morning sun kissed the tops of the skyscrapers on the Upper West Side of Manhattan. In Jason's bedroom, on the twenty-third floor of an art-deco apartment building, Jason and Nathalie were asleep.

Jason was under the comforter; all you could see was his tussled black hair. Next to him lay Nathalie, her head buried in the goose-down pillow. Poppy was curled up like a Danish pastry between them.

The slumbering silence was broken by the sound of the phone. Poppy sprang to life and barked hysterically. Jason woke and fumbled first for his glasses, then for the receiver.

"Yeah?"

It was the producer of *News Hour*, and what he said had an electric effect on Jason, who sat bolt upright.

"What? It's happening today? God, this is incredible! . . . Sure, I'll be there! I'll be at the airport in thirty minutes!"

He put down the phone and leapt from the bed. The dog was still barking, shaking in paroxysms of agonized yelps.

"Shut up, Poppy!"

What was wrong with this friggin' dog? Jason secretly dreamed of, one day, taking her to the vet and having her vocal chords removed, or, better still, just throwing her out the window. He could tell Nathalie she had gotten out onto the ledge, and been blown off by a gust of wind. He remembered, fondly, a story they'd had on *News Hour* about a chihuahua, out for a walk with its owner, who'd been plucked off the ground and swallowed whole by a pelican.

Nathalie opened her eyes. She'd been dreaming she was being chased across a beach by a giant cheeseburger. She shuddered, glad to be awake.

"Jason?"

Jason was at the closet, yanking out a suit.

"Jason? What are you doing?"

"Sorry, honey, I've got to go. The Martians are landing in Nevada! Can you believe it? I just got a call from the office. I've gotta get down there. They want me to cover it."

At the sound of Nathalie's voice, Poppy had, thankfully, stopped barking, and now was wagging her tail and licking Nathalie's face.

"Look, there's stuff in the fridge, okay? I'm

sorry, but, you understand. It's my job. I'll call you later. You go back to sleep."

"Nevada?" said Nathalie, groggy. "What, Vegas?"

"No, a place called Pahrump. It's out in the desert." Jason was standing in his underwear, buttoning up his shirt. He looked at the rack. Should he wear his Harvard tie?

In the bed, Nathalie pushed Poppy away.

"But we had plans . . . there's that sale at Barney's."

"Nathalie, you've got to learn to prioritize!"

Jason slung the tie around his neck. Now, what kind of shoes? The desert—it was pretty rough terrain—he could wear those Doc Martins he got in London.

The phone rang again.

"I'll get it. It's probably for me," said Jason.

Nathalie got there first.

"Hello?"

She sat up. Jason hovered behind her.

"It's for me," she said.

"Who is it? Who knows you're here?"

She waved him away, listening intently.

"Yeah, I've heard," she said.

Jason, aggravated, returned to dressing.

"I guess I could move a few things around," she said.

Who was she talking to?

"Okay, baby, *ciao*." She hung up the phone, wide awake now, and turned to Jason with a grin. "That was the network. We're *both* going! It's a 'His and Her's' Martian landing!"

Jason's face fell. How did she do it? Plums just dropped in her lap! It wasn't fair. She hadn't even finished high school. Okay, so she was cute, so what?

"Isn't this exciting?" cried Nathalie, jumping up and down on the bed. "Hey!"

Jason scowled at her. "Could you stop being delightfully uninhibited for a moment? I'm trying to get ready!"

Chapter 14

The bay-trees in our country are all wither'd
And meteors fright the fixed stars of heaven;
The pale-fac'd moon looks bloody on the earth,
And lean-look'd prophets whisper fearful change;
Rich men look sad and ruffians dance and leap,
The one in fear to lose what they enjoy,
The other to enjoy by rage and war;
These signs forerun the death or fall of kings.

—William Shakespeare,
Richard II

Six miles southeast of the small desert town of Pahrump, nothing was happening. This was normal. Nothing had happened here since the Mesozoic Period, when a diplodicus had an argument with a stegosaurus over a fern. The conflict did not benefit either party. They exchanged a few blows and trampled the fern into the dirt.

Now, a few hundred millennia later, on the

GREAT MOVIE ACTION
FROM SIGNET

☐ **UNSTRUNG HEROES by Franz Lidz.** Meet the Uncles Lidz: Danny, a paranoid who's convinced Mickey Mantle is trying to kill him; Leo, the self-proclaimed Messiah of Washington Heights; Harry, who claims the world crown in nine boxing divisions; and Arthur, who has amassed North America's premier collection of used shoelaces. Each plays an integral part in this true and truly crazy story of a boy's life amid the looniest of families. (184424—$4.99)

☐ **A WALK IN THE CLOUDS by Deborah Chiel, based on a screenplay by Robert Mark Kamen.** Paul Sutton and Victoria Aragon came from different worlds. They met each other in the wrong place at the wrong time in the wrong way. Yet their passion grew, fed by the magical power of the harvest tradition. Amidst the lush vines of a Napa Valley winery and the love and loyalty of a fiercely proud family, it seemed anything was possible. (185935—$4.99)

☐ **A LITTLE PRINCESS by Frances Hodgson Burnett.** Here, in one of the best-loved children's stories in the world, we follow the adventures of the irrepressible Sara as she introduces us to a series of unforgettable characters . . . the perpetually cross Miss Minchin . . . the spirited and infinitely loving Large family . . . the warm-hearted scullery maid, Becky. And when a mysterious Indian gentleman moves into the house next door, Sara's life is transformed once again. (526228—$3.95)

☐ **DON JUAN DE MARCO by Jean Blake White, based on the screenplay by Jeremy Leven.** A young patient claims he is Don Juan, the world's greatest lover. A seasoned psychiatrist has only 10 days before he retires in order to set him straight. But is the doctor prepared for the breathtaking tale of Don Juan's life? (184394—$4.99)

*Prices slightly higher in Canada

JONATHAN GEMS was born in London, England, the son of Pam and Keith Gems. A playwright, he had ten plays produced during the 1980s, including: *The Tax Exile*, *Naked Robots*, and *Susan's Breasts*. He performed writing services for the film of George Orwell's *1984* and *White Mischief*, directed by Michael Radford; wrote and directed *The Dress*, which won Best Film at the Aspen Short Film Festival, and wrote the screenplay *Mars Attacks* for Tim Burton. His play *The Paranormalist* recently opened at the Complex Theater in Los Angeles, and he is about to direct his first full-length movie, *The Treat*, starring Andrew McCarthy. He currently lives in Los Angeles.

place where the fern once stood, grew a small cactus. The loudest thing this cactus had ever heard was the noise of sandflies beating their wings. None of the desert flora or fauna was prepared for what was coming.

It began with the low, jagged, throbbing sound of a dozen military helicopters. They appeared dramatically from behind the sand dunes, soaring through the bright blue sky.

Two miles behind them, a division of army vehicles sped across the scrub. In the front jeep, General Casey was standing, talking into a military phone.

"I get to greet the Martian ambassador! Isn't that great?"

He was talking to his wife back in Richmond, Virginia. He always kept her abreast of developments. She was a wonderful wife, even more interested in his career than he was. Her father had been a military man and she knew the whole gameboard.

She was a great asset in every way except one; she couldn't have children. But this suited Bill Casey just fine—he didn't want to compete with a bunch of children. Bill was still a child himself. Bill had played with toy soldiers as a boy. Now the soldiers were real, that was the only difference. He treated life as play, which was probably why he was so successful.

His wife congratulated him on his important commission. "Yeah, it's one hell of an honor. Didn't I always tell you, honey, if I stayed in line and didn't speak up, good things would happen?"

"Yes, you did, sweetie."

"I think, after this, I might get a fourth star."

"That would be wonderful! Oh, did you remember to take your antihistamine?"

"Shoot! I forgot."

"You know about your allergies," scolded his wife.

"Yes, but I left the pills in the car. I had so many things to think about. I've got a whole division here . . ."

"That's okay, sweetie," said his wife. "But if you feel your allergies acting up, you just send out one of those recruits to go get your pills, okay?"

"Okay, sugar-lump. Listen, I'd better go. I can see the landing site. Now, you be sure to watch me on TV, okay?"

"You bet I will, huggy-bear, and I'm gonna tape it, too!"

From the easterly direction, on Highway 160, a line of cars was moving at quite a lick. Word had leaked out that Martians were going to land near Pahrump, and these people wanted to be there. There were all sorts: UFO-watchers, New-

Age hippies, crystal-gazers, astrologers, Branch Davidians, dolphin-swimmers, Freemen, Trek-kies, ravers, and lots of retired senior citizens in RVs. Cars, trucks, and RVs lined the highway for a mile and a half.

Midway down the line was Barbara Land in a dark blue Mercedes. Beside her on the passenger seat was her collection of crystals and sticks of incense.

Looking at all the vehicles ahead and behind her, she anticipated the landing site would be overcrowded and decided to find a vantage point where she could watch the Martian landing alone. She sensed that the Martians would bring a powerful energy with them and she needed a place to meditate, to get centered—the better to experience it.

At the landing site, the helicopters had touched down. Soldiers were erecting barriers around the perimeter of a circular area two hundred yards in diameter. At the center of this circle was the point described by the coordinates received by the tracking station in New Mexico. At this spot, a squad of soldiers were laying down a canvas sheet on which was painted, in letters four feet high, WELCOME TO EARTH!

At the north side of the perimeter, a band-stand was being constructed. One of those toil-

ing on it was Private Billy-Glenn Norris. A short distance away, in front of a row of army tents, the band of the 17th Marine Regiment were tuning up. All around the perimeter, soldiers were hammering in fence posts.

Parked just outside the perimeter were army vehicles—tanks, half tracks, armored trucks, jeeps, tractor trailers, motorcycles, and military caravans. An HQ had been hastily set up in a large bell-tent situated next to the tank park.

General Casey came out of the HQ, accompanied by two colonels.

"There's a lot riding on this. The whole world is watching. I want your men to be at their parade-ground best."

The two colonels both nodded. "Yessir!"

Describing a second circle outside the perimeter was a barrier made of roadblocks, where Marine guards were stationed at ten-yard intervals. Their job was to welcome the official civilian guests and to keep out the riffraff.

A steady stream of people arriving, representing countries from all over the world. Nathalie and Jason arrived in tandem; Jason in front, in the General News Networks truck, Nathalie tailgating in the shocking-pink "Fashion TV" motor home. They showed their passes to the guards and were waved through.

General Casey, flanked by the two colonels,

conducted an inspection of the camp. They passed a row of jeeps and came upon a group of men in white coats gathered around a computer mounted on an airport baggage trailer. Nearby was the tow tractor that would move the computer to whichever location was desired. Casey recognized Dr. Herman Ziegler. "Hello, Doctor, how's it going?"

"Very good."

"Are you positive it's going to work?"

"Positively positive," said Ziegler. "The new programs I have downloaded can recognize and translate any sequence of sounds, any language patterns."

"Good," said Casey. "We don't want any slipups."

On a hill overlooking the landing site, Barbara Land found the perfect spot. She laid her Indian blanket on the ground, and began to arrange her crystals.

Between the barrier and the perimeter fence, the news media and special guests made themselves comfortable. The army had thoughtfully provided camp chairs and a buffet service.

Jason was standing on the roof of the GNN truck, speaking into the camera, operated by his bearded buddy, Ronny.

"The teeming masses are gathered here . . ."

he said ". . . from who knows how many states . . . watching and waiting."

A few yards away, on top of the pink "Fashion TV" motor home, Nathalie, her chihuahua held in the crook of her arm, was also talking into camera.

The flotilla of vehicles that had been pouring down Highway 160 had now arrived, creating a carnival atmosphere outside the barrier. Jason could see families setting up their own little campsites, wandering the barrier, talking excitedly, making new friends and sharing conspiracy theories. His attention was especially caught by the sight of a nine-year-old boy dressed in a discount-store Martian costume, which included a beanie with two antennae.

"Why have they come?" continued Jason to the camera. "Curiosity? Or something more? Hope for change? For progress? For experience? For something to tell their grandchildren? Or, just to say: 'I was there. I was there when first man met with Martian.' This is Jason Stone, GNN, Pahrump."

The red light on the camera blinked out. Jason relaxed.

"Was that all right for you?"

Ronny nodded. "Perfect."

On the top of her bluff, overlooking the scene, Barbara meditated. The sounds of the sightseers,

the army, and the Marines faded away. She could sense the white energy of the crystals and she could smell the fragrance of the desert, mingling with the scent of her incense. Time stood still.

It could have been two minutes or two hours later when Barbara heard it—a strange swishing sound. This unusual sound broke through into her alpha state. As she felt herself coming back into her body, the eager hubbub of the crowd became audible, and she heard a voice cry:

"They're here!"

Opening her eyes she saw an honest-to-goodness flying saucer hovering a few hundred feet above the landing site. It resembled a giant aluminum Frisbee with indented markings around its rim, and seemed to be about a block and a half in diameter. There was a faint doppling effect, as if it were changing the chemicals in the air around it. The swishing sound seemed to come from the spaceship's rapid spinning.

Everyone stared up at the spacecraft that was blocking out the sun. General Casey wondered why it had stopped there. Why wasn't it landing?

He tore his eyes away, surveyed the landing site, and saw the problem. Inside the perimeter fence, parked in a ring at regular intervals, were the helicopters. There wasn't enough space. The

flying saucer was too big. The choppers would have to go. He clicked on his walkie-talkie and spoke to the squadron commander.

In the crowd, inside and outside the barrier, guests and tourists were taking pictures and videoing the flying saucer. Over by the bandstand, Billy-Glenn gazed at the silver spaceship in awe. He couldn't wait to tell Meg about this!

The helicopter pilots were all in their cockpits, awaiting instructions. General Casey spoke into his radio: "Give 'em room," he ordered.

Amid swirling dust, the helicopters lifted off, rising in a ring above the gleaming spacecraft. It looked like a kind of aerial ballet. A few moments passed, then the massive saucer slowly began to descend. As it neared the ground, its spinning slowed and the swishing sound gave way to a high-pitched whine. More clouds of dust flew up and soldiers and civilians covered their faces.

On the underside of the saucer, hatches slid open and six crablike metal legs mechanically unfolded. The spinning slowed to a complete stop. The high-pitched whine faded out and the saucer floated lightly to the ground.

The onlookers were hushed with anticipation. General Casey was the first one to break the silence. Switching his radio frequency to the Pen-

tagon channel, he depressed the 'transmit' button.

"The egg is in the nest," he said. "I repeat, the egg is in the nest."

Holding his microphone to his chest, Jason signaled to Ronny and stepped in front of the camera.

Across the way, on top of the motor home, Nathalie did the same thing. "I wish you were here with me now," she said, straight into the camera. The wind whipped at her hair. She held it back with her left hand.

"You can see behind me the giant spaceship, glinting in the Nevada sun like a giant hubcap. This is the most amazing thing I have ever seen."

In the Oval Office, the President, the First Lady, Taffy, General Decker, Jerry Ross, and Professor Kessler were glued to the television. The President was couch commander, having possession of the remote control. The White House satellite TV system provided three hundred channels from around the world and the President was surfing. He wanted to know how the event was being seen by the foreign news media. He stopped on the Pakistani channel. The Pakistani reporter, wearing a dark suit and a turban, was saying: "The flying machine has

landed. It resembles very much a giant silver chapati."

The President clicked to another channel. Here a French reporter was waving his arms.

"And here it is, the marvelous spaceship from Mars! Of course, many people in France have seen these before—but now it is the turn of the Americans."

He clicked again. An English reporter was on the screen. "Apparently, extraterrestrial life may be making an appearance here in the United States. We are told the visitors are from the planet Mars—well, that may be true, but then again, it may not."

At the landing site, a sharp sound came from the flying saucer. The crowd murmured. Nathalie, atop the "Fashion TV" motor home, spoke into her microphone. "Something is happening!"

There was a rasping of gears and a door slid open in the rim of the spacecraft. Then a bright metallic ramp flowed out, extending downward.

"A ramp is emerging like a silver tongue," said Jason, to camera.

"Gee whiz," General Casey said, as the ramp reached the ground and stopped.

A moment passed and then a small, strangely garbed figure appeared in the doorway. It was

the same creature that many had seen on their televisions—the Martian ambassador. He was wearing a transparent dome over his megacephalic head, a rubberlike suit and breathing apparatus. He started down the ramp. And, after him, marching in pairs, came twelve Martian warriors. The crowd gasped.

Via the TV cameras, over a billion people, all over the world, saw the first Martians to arrive on Earth.

Nathalie spoke urgently into her microphone. "The Martians are wearing tightly fitted green space suits with, what looks like, Plexiglas domes over their heads. The Martian ambassador looks very dashing in an almost fluorescent peacock-blue cape, fastened at the neck with a high, curling collar . . ."

General Casey gestured to his two colonels. They had rehearsed this moment. The 24th Army Regiment and the 17th Marine Corps Regiment snapped to attention and the Marine band struck up "The Star-Spangled Banner."

The Martians came down off the ramp and spread out in a line facing the regiments. Beyond the barrier, people watched through binoculars, telescopes, and the zoom lenses of their cameras. On her hill, Barbara watched, goggle-eyed.

General Casey hopped forward and extended

his hand. The Martian ambassador stepped back, folded his arms and glared at him with such malevolence that Casey felt the hair prickle on the back of his neck. He had clearly offended the Martian somehow. Casey looked at the two colonels for help. They both shrugged; neither of them knew what to do. They'd never been in a situation like this before.

Then Casey had an inspiration. He turned to the Martian ambassador and, bowing slightly, drew a large circle in the air.

The Martian ambassador relaxed, took a step forward, and began to speak. The sounds he made were screeches, grunts, and ducklike quacks. The soldiers, standing at attention, tried not to wince. Dr. Ziegler ran up beside General Casey.

"Wait, wait—one second, please!"

Behind him came his white-coated assistants on the tractor, towing the computer equipment. The Martian ambassador stopped talking, watching the activity of the scientists with a red, fishy eye.

Ziegler pressed some buttons and the sounds made by the alien emissary reverberated, painfully, from the speakers. None of the Martians moved a muscle.

Trembling, Ziegler pressed another button and the whole world heard the babbling shriek

of tape rewinding with the volume up. "Sorry," said Ziegler, and turned the volume down. Then the German linguist punched another button and the synthesized voice of the computer, with its spooky, hollow echo, said: "Greetings! I am the Martian ambassador." Dr. Ziegler turned proudly to Casey.

"Everything is in phase, General. You may speak."

Casey nodded and took a deep breath. "Greetings! I am General Casey, Commanding Officer in the Armed Forces of the United States of America. On behalf of the people of Earth—Welcome!"

In the Oval Office, the President, the First Lady, Taffy, Professor Kessler, and Jerry Ross were pleased.

"He did that well," said Jerry.

"Yes, he did," agreed the President.

General Decker looked away and sneered.

At the desert landing site, Dr. Ziegler translated General Casey into Martian. The crowd waited expectantly as the computer spat out the Martian argot. The skull-faced ambassador quickly replied.

The synthesized voice blared out what the ambassador had said: "We come in peace. We come in peace! We come in peace!"

General Casey beamed. On her hill, Barbara grinned from ear to ear. The kid wearing the alien beanie blew his whistle. Everyone clapped and cheered. Even the soldiers applauded. A handsome, bearded hippie, dressed like Jesus, pulled out a white dove from under his tunic.

"They came in peace!" he cried, in ecstasy, and tossed the dove into the air. Applause thundered around the landing site as the white dove flew toward the spaceship. The Martian ambassador saw the bird coming, bared his teeth, and hissed. One of the Martians pulled a raygun from his holster and—Pzzzzzttt!—the dove instantly exploded.

Suddenly the Martian ambassador had a gun in his hand. Whooosh! He blew a hole the size of a dinner plate in General Casey's stomach!

All the Martians started firing! Dr. Ziegler and the two colonels were totally disintegrated! More Martians poured down the ramp. Some of them, with firearms shaped like tennis rackets, shot light-rings at the tanks, which all exploded, sending a storm of razor-sharp shrapnel through the troops.

The soldiers ran. The hippie was cut in half by a proton beam. The kid with the alien beanie was vaporized. The guests crashed through the barriers and joined the spectators, who were dashing to their vehicles, falling over each other

in a mad scramble to escape. Death rays cut them down, like wheat before a scythe.

Throughout the United States, and the rest of the world, people watched what later became known as the "Pahrump Massacre," live on their TV sets.

The helicopters wheeled and dove toward the killing zone, firing their machine guns at the Martians below. They responded by training their bizarre weapons on the helicopter fleet and blowing them out of the sky. A Martian fired a bazooka-like tube, shooting an emerald fireball at the Marine Corps band. The bandstand burst apart in a sickening green flash.

Billy-Glenn Norris aimed his sidearm at the nearest Martian. "Die, you alien shithead!" he shouted, and pulled the trigger.

Pow! His bullet bounced off the green body armor of its target, and the Martian swiveled, his red eyes blazing.

"Uh-oh."

He had to think of something quick! Bullets were no use. On the ground lay an American flag. Billy-Glenn snatched it up and waved it at the Martian.

"Look, this is the flag. It's yours. I surrender, okay?"

The Martian didn't fire.

This is going to work! thought Billy-Glenn.

Way across the scenes of carnage, Ronny, the GNN cameraman, was still filming. The ear-splitting noise and the destruction around him, had so confused him that he was working on automatic pilot. He panned his camera just as Billy-Glenn offered the flag to the Martian, catching the moment when the Martian blew Billy-Glenn into a thousand pieces!

On the roof of the "Fashion TV" motor home, Nathalie clutched Poppy to her chest. Boom! Ring fire hit the motor home. For a second, Nathalie was conscious of flying through the air. Then everything went black.

The ground was shuddering with the impact of a massive exchange of fire. The soldiers were trying to fight back. Running low, under a latticework of multicolored flame, Jason sped to where Nathalie lay, spread-eagled like a broken doll.

"Nathalie! Nathalie!" he shouted above the din.

Was she dead? He knelt down beside her and took her limp hand. An explosion blew a crater in the ground only yards from where Jason was kneeling. Miraculously, Nathalie opened her eyes. Jason gasped.

"Thank God!"

He clasped her hand tightly. A Martian appeared through the smoke and fired his raygun.

Pzzzzttt! Jason's clothes and flesh evaporated from his body! Nathalie, too shocked to scream, was left holding Jason's severed hand! She fainted.

A few moments later, Poppy trotted over to the hand, picked it up in her mouth, and ran off to find a place to bury it.

All around the landing site, Martians were slaughtering humans. A Marine sergeant, hit by a raygun blast, fell, his machine gun in his hands. Dying, he squeezed off a few rounds. One of them hit a Martian's dome. It cracked open and the bullet smashed into his brain. The dome filled with green gas and, squeaking and staggering, the Martian collapsed. The sergeant died, but not in vain. He had found a weak spot in the Martian enemy. Their body armor was bullet-proof and their weapons were superior, but you could kill them if you shot them in the head.

By now, the tanks and armored cars were destroyed, the trucks, jeeps, and trailers were mangled and burning. The desert was scattered with the burning carcasses of helicopters and civilian motor vehicles. And the Martians were using their deadly accurate long-range weapons to mop up the fleeing stragglers.

Groups of ghoulish skull-men strolled among the dead, picking up mementos. One Martian

retrieved the scorched carcass of the dove. Another picked up a lady's purse and put it in a bag. The Martian ambassador motioned for a group of his soldiers to carry the unconscious Nathalie up the ramp into the spaceship.

Elsewhere, Poppy, still with Jason's hand in her mouth, went up to a Martian and wiggled. The Martian took the hand and placed it in a bag. Then he picked up Poppy.

A few of the cameras were still running, even though their operators were now dust in the wind. Throughout the world, viewers were openmouthed in front of their TV sets.

In Perkinsville, Kansas, Glenn and Sue-Ann Norris were traumatized.

In Richmond, Virginia, Janet Casey had tears rolling down her cheeks. She had taped the death of her husband!

In Las Vegas, in the sports bar, Byron, Cindy, everyone was in shock. No one had seen so much killing done so quickly.

On the hill, overlooking the battlefield, Barbara tried to quell the spasms of grief that shook her body. Her eyes were too flooded with tears to see the Martian ambassador march up the ramp, followed by his troops. She was too impacted by the horror of the thousands of scorched corpses, to notice the ramp retract, the door close, and the saucer levitate. She didn't

hear the high-pitched whine, nor did she see the flying saucer zoom straight up and vanish into the blue Nevada sky.

"Holy Moses!' said the First Lady.

"Did you see that?" said Jerry to no one in particular.

In the Oval Office, the President and his group were devastated. General Decker stood up. "Mr. President, it is my formal recommendation that we hit these assholes with everything we've got!"

The President was too dazed to speak. Kessler, agitated, got up from the couch and started waving his pipe.

"Sir, I know this is terrible, but please, please, don't be rash. Did you see how they reacted to that dove? It definitely frightened them."

"Nuke 'em!" urged Decker.

"We must establish communication!" insisted Kessler.

"Why don't we set up a Town Hall?" suggested Jerry. "We'll get the public's opinion."

The President turned desperately to his wife. "What do you think, Marsha?"

"I think we should kick the living crap out of them."

Decker pointed to her, nodding his head enthusiastically.

"But, but this could all be, be, a cultural mis-understanding!" Kessler stammered.

"Yeah," said Taffy. "Maybe on Mars, doves mean war?"

Everyone in the room mulled this over.

Chapter 15

For Death we all are nurtured,
The greatest and the least.
Like fatted pigs for slaughter,
To die as dies the beast.

—Palladas of Alexandria

Outside the Luxor Hotel, on the Las Vegas Strip, a newspaper vending machine was being loaded. On the front page of the *Las Vegas Examiner* howled the headline: MARS TRAGEDY. Below, was a photo of Billy-Glenn holding the American flag, just as he was hit by the fatal raygun blast. Photographed through the smoke, the image had a mythic, heroic, Iwo Jima quality.

In the Anubis Lounge, customers were watching the TV over the bar, which was playing footage of the Pahrump Massacre. A male newscaster was speaking in voice-over. "Two entire regiments were wiped out, including

General Bill Casey, the operation commander, Colonel Antonio Guevera, Colonel James Wilson, the celebrated linguist, Dr. Herman Ziegler, GNN reporter Jason Stone, FTV reporter Nathalie West, British journalist Simon Mudeford, the French news anchor Jean-Claude Bonet, twelve diplomats from the United Nations . . ."

In the casino, the noise of the slot machines was out of control. At the overcrowded roulette, craps, keno, blackjack, and baccarat tables, people were shrieking at the tops of their voices. Everyone had gambling fever.

Over at the five-cent slots, the elderly white-haired lady, with her white plastic bucket of nickels, had commandeered three machines. She was wearing a new, extra-large T-shirt. It displayed the now famous photo of Billy-Glenn holding the America flag and the words: AMERICAN HERO.

Byron Williams, in his pharoah costume, was having his picture taken with three Chinese gentlemen.

"Thank you, thank you! You are the greatest champ ever!"

"Number One left hook!"

"Thanks. You're very kind," said Byron graciously.

The Chinese gentlemen bowed and hurried

away. Byron spotted Cindy going by with a heavily loaded tray of drinks.

"Hey, Cindy, how's it going?"

She grinned. "Isn't this great? I always get huge tips during national disasters!"

Byron smiled and watched her speed away on her high heels. Then he looked at the frenzy around him. Was it him? Or was the world totally crazy?

In the White House Radio Room, a nerdy technician, wearing headphones, sat at a transmitter. Beside him was a computer, a twin to the one obliterated at the landing site. Professor Kessler and a weary President Dale stood over him.

"Right, let's do it," said the President. "I know we're making the right decision."

The nerdy tech pressed a button and the computer tapes turned. "Ready to transmit, sir," he said. Dale spoke into the microphone. "This is the President of the United States . . ."

He glanced at the script in his hand. "I'm speaking to you in the hope that what happened earlier today was a cultural misunderstanding. There is no doubt that we two species have a lot to offer one another. . . ."

In Colorado, twenty miles west of Estes Park, a large satellite dish was pointing at the sky,

transmitting the President's message to the Martian flagship.

"You must be as excited as we are to find intelligent life in this solar system. And let me make one thing clear: you have nothing to fear from us. Our customs may be strange to you, but we mean no harm. So let us sit down together in friendship. . . ."

In the Martian flagship, in a pearl-colored, vaulted, high-tech chamber, a Martian communications officer wrote down the President's message. Then he got up and walked straight into the wall. The wall, reacting to his body heat, changed its molecular structure, and allowed him to pass through.

He was now at one end of an immensely long specimen chamber. He walked past a row of giant glass eggs containing biological specimens from Earth: a cow, a giant squid, a pig, a sheep, a clown, a camel, and Nathalie West, in her bra and underwear, holding her chihuahua.

He ambled past a group of scientists from his hometown of Grckkhlftttpt. They were examining the charred remains of the dove, poking at it with a thin metal rod. He made a left turn and stepped through the wall, entering the control center.

Here, the Martian leader was reclining on his throne, leafing through a copy of *Playboy*. He

was fascinated by the fleshy protuberances on the sternum area of "Miss April."

The communications officer saluted and clicked his tongue. The Martian leader looked up, bade him speak, and listened to his report. Then he dismissed him with a sound similar to that of a burp.

Chapter 16

"Dark is the suede that mows like a harvest."

—The Martian Ambassador

Barbara stood at the edge of her illuminated pool. The night had grown chilly, but she didn't want to go in. She didn't want to move ever again. Her arms wrapped around herself, she stood, as motionless as a stone, staring into the water. She heard the distant sound of dogs barking and the occasional car horn. But she wasn't interested in traffic or dogs. Only one thing seemed real, and that was Death.

Was there really such a thing as meaning? People always want stuff to mean something—why? Maybe because it gave them the illusion and security of control? But Barbara knew the truth. The Universe was meaningless. Death ruled.

Inside the house a door slammed. It was Art, back from work. She wanted to talk to him. She had never wanted to talk to him so badly as now. The problem was, she couldn't remember when, or if, they had ever really talked. Did they, when they first met? She vaguely recalled finding a neglected softness in him that offered communication, but, throughout the years of their marriage, he had not opened up. In fact, he had withdrawn. When, three months ago, she'd given up drinking, she tried, with all her might, to connect with him. But it was too late. Art simply wasn't interested in her anymore.

Barbara looked through the floor-to-ceiling glass windows into the back living room. She could see him moving around. She hadn't told him she'd gone to the Martian landing. She wondered if he'd heard about the massacre? Her eye fell on a bottle of Cristal champagne on the glass shelf by the door.

Art was pacing in front of the fireplace, talking into a Dictaphone. "When the investors fly in, I want a limo waiting for each one of 'em. And make sure every car is top-of-the-line, with leather interiors."

Barbara entered the living room with the face of someone who has seen The End.

"Art, are you still spinning your wheels on

that cockamamie hotel? Get real! The Martians are going to attack! It's all over!"

Art glanced at her. He had a question.

"Barbara, what do you think? Do kids bring their parents to Vegas, or do the parents bring the kids? Who drives the decision?"

As usual, he hadn't heard her.

"Didn't you hear me?" she said. "Did you see what happened? You know what I'm talking about, right?"

"Yeah, the Martian thing. Sure, I know all about it. It was a cultural misunderstanding—don't worry about it."

"Art, listen to me, please! I was there! I saw it! That wasn't a cultural misunderstanding! They're going to kill us!"

"You were there? What are you talking about? You weren't there. They killed everybody there. Jesus! Don't go nutsy on me now, that's all I need."

"I was there."

"No you weren't."

"They want to kill us all!"

"Barbara, why don't you go and take one of your pills? I got work to do."

"But what's the point when the Martians are going to destroy everything?"

"Okay, so we got a few things to straighten out with these guys, I know that, but, hey, they

come to Earth, they need a place to stay, same as anybody else. And I'm gonna give it to 'em!"

"Oh my God," said Barbara. "I got sober for this? We're finished. We're doomed! We're *doomed*!" She grabbed the bottle of Cristal and swept out.

Art watched her go and clicked on his Dictaphone.

"That reminds me. Stock every limo with a bottle of Cristal."

In the White House Radio Room, Professor Kessler and the nerdy technician were waiting for a message from space. Neither of them was speaking.

Since the Pahrump Massacre, Kessler had been feeling lousy. The death of Nathalie West, announced on the news, had thrown him into a mood of angry depression.

He couldn't blame the Martians for her death because, logically, their actions made no sense. If they were hostile, they would have attacked. After all, they had a fleet of several thousand vehicles in orbit around the Earth. Obviously, something had happened at Pahrump to scare them. They'd reacted out of fear. It was just unlucky that Nathalie had been there.

He felt more irate at the TV company for

sending her. What did she need to go there for? She was a fashion journalist, for heaven's sake!

He didn't want to talk to anybody. He was content to be hiding in the Radio Room waiting for the Martians to respond to the President's communiqué.

For his part, the nerdy technician would have liked to talk with the great professor, but the guy seemed to be in a really gnarly mood.

All at once, the radio equipment sprang to life. Lights flashed and there was a burst of static. Martian lingo sputtered out of the speakers. Kessler perked up.

"They're responding!" said the nerdy tech.

The computer was already recording and translating the message.

Sometime later, on the third floor, the President, dressed in striped flannel pajamas, was in his private bathroom. He was brushing his teeth and getting ready for bed. There was a knock.

"Mr. President?" It was the voice of Mitch, the Secret Service man.

"What is it?"

"It's Mr. Ross, sir."

"Okay, send him in."

The door opened and Jerry entered cautiously. "Hello, James, I think it's good news."

"About time," the President mumbled, brushing his teeth.

"We just got a message from the Martians."

"Yeah? What's it say?"

Jerry looked at his friend with warmth. He loved to be the bearer of good news. Dale could be a dull son of a bitch, but he had plucked Jerry from a going-nowhere job on public radio to elevate him to his current exalted status. No one had ever done anything so nice for Jerry Ross.

"They've issued a formal apology," he said.

The President wiped his face with a towel. "Didn't I tell you this would happen?"

"Yeah. Listen to this . . ." Jerry read aloud from the paper given to him by Kessler: "The Martian ambassador feels terrible, and asks permission to speak to Congress." He looked up at his friend.

"They want to speak to Congress, huh?" said the President.

"That's good, isn't it?"

"You bet! You know what this is, Jerry? It's a major victory for our administration. Okay, get out of the bathroom, I gotta do a potty."

Chapter 17

Art is meant to disturb,
Science reassures.

—Georges Braques

The next morning found Donald Kessler, with a group of colleagues, doing an alien autopsy.

A year earlier he had been given the new Ross Perot Annex to the Science Building at Georgetown University for his own personal use. It was a great honor for one of America's premier research scientists, but it hadn't been a shoe-in. He'd had to beat out some stiff competition.

What gave him the edge was his special relationship with the current management at the White House.

His first girlfriend, Georgina Helwig-Larsen, an ambitious grant scholar, once told him the key to success. "There are three prerequisites,"

she had told him. "One: you need a product, skill, or talent, that is, something to offer. Two: you need to know the right people. Three: you need to look the part."

Donald Kessler had followed her three precepts religiously. He had worked hard to become a leading expert in several fields of science, he had refined his image, and he had made friends in high places. As a result, he triumphed over his competitors.

Kessler leaned over and peered into the central cortex of the semidissected Martian's brain. It looked like pulpy red cabbage. Despite his oxygen mask, he almost gagged from the foul odor.

Two Martian cadavers had been retrieved from the Nevada landing site. The one they were working on was the best specimen. The other had been shot in the head with a high-velocity bullet, destroying everything above the eyebrows.

Surrounding the operating table, and watching Kessler's explorations, were three top surgeons, two biologists, a biochemist, and a vet.

Kessler poked inside the Martian's brain, moving tissues with the tip of his scalpel.

"You see the highly developed cranial nerve system?" murmured Kessler.

"This explains the unusual cerebral arteries."

The other men nodded and grunted.

"And we seem to have several glands here, beneath the optic chiasm."

"Very curious," said one of the surgeons.

At the same time, in Space, in the Martian flagship, three Martian scientists were gathered around a tall, tilted structure similar to a chair.

Strapped into this structure was the body of Nathalie West, still dressed in bra and panties. All over her body, thin, multicolored tubes sprouted out of her skin, snaking and curling to various incomprehensible machines.

On a work surface across the room, in a large glass jar, was Nathalie's head, also fed by the mysterious tubes. The head blinked and its eyes moved. Nathalie's head was alive!

The scientists moved away from the chair-structure, revealing that the head of Poppy, the chihuahua, had been grafted on to Nathalie's neck. One of the Martian scientists turned to a trolley and selected a pair of circuit grips that were connected by wires to a battery. He attached the grips to the big toes of Nathalie's body's feet. Electricity buzzed through her body and Poppy's head barked!

Across the room, in the jar, Nathalie's head screamed!

Chapter 18

"Love's a malady without a cure."

—John Dryden

In Perkinsville, in the Veterans' Association cemetery across the street from the First Baptist Church, a somber military funeral was in progress.

Surrounding a freshly dug grave, were the Norris family, shoulder to shoulder with high-ranking military officers. Encircling them was a crowd of strangers, many of them wearing T-shirts emblazoned with the Iwo Jima picture of Billy-Glenn. Dotted among them were members of the news media, filming and taking pictures.

An army bugler played "Taps" as the coffin, draped in the American flag, was lowered into the grave. The priest crossed himself. Billy-Glenn's girlfriend, Meg, burst into tears. Sue-

Ann turned her face away. Richie stood help-lessly. Glenn Norris shook his head, distraught.

"Why'd it have to be him?" he said.

"Imagine . . . dying while fighting for our flag!" said one of the strangers, awed by the so-lemnity of the event.

"There ain't many heroes," said another.

Richie looked around at the crowd. "Who *are* these people?" he whispered.

In Washington, D.C., Louise Williams was mak-ing breakfast. Her sons were in the living room playing a violent video game on the TV. The phone rang. Louise answered it. It was Byron.

"Byron! Is everything all right?" she said. "You still coming tomorrow?"

"Try and stop me. The plane gets in at four."

"That's fine. The boys can't wait to see you."

Byron was in the bedroom of his condo. Out of the window could be seen the pyramid-shaped Luxor Hotel. He sat on the windowsill wondering if he had the nerve to ask her.

"How about you? Do *you* want to see me?"

Louise smiled. "I can think of worse things than seeing your ugly mug again."

Byron felt his shoulders relax. "Are the kids there?"

"Yeah, hold on." Louise called the boys. "Your dad's on the phone!"

Cedric and Neville jumped up, the video game immediately forgotten.

"Me first!" shouted Cedric.

"No, me! Me!" yelled Neville.

They scrambled into the kitchen. Neville got to the phone first.

"Hey, Dad!"

"Who's that? Neville?"

"Yeah."

"How's it going?"

"Okay."

"You taking care of your mother and being a good boy?"

"Yeah. Hey, Dad, guess what? We're going to the White House!"

"You're going to the White House?"

Cedric grabbed the phone from his brother and pushed him away.

"Yeah—tomorrow!" said Cedric.

"Hey, give it back!" complained Neville.

"It's a school thing," said Cedric. "Like a tour."

"So, I guess this means you're still making it to school once in a while?"

Cedric chuckled. "Yeah!"

"Cedric, gimme your mother again."

Cedric held the phone up above his head to stop Neville from grabbing it. "Ma!"

Louise came over from the kitchen table, wiping her hands. She took the phone.

"What you wasting this phone time for? This is expensive. We're seeing you tomorrow."

Byron thrilled to the sound of her voice.

"Yeah, okay, baby, I just want to say something to you 'cause I feel like saying it."

"What's that?"

"I love you."

"I love you, too, Byron—now, stop wasting money. I'll see you tomorrow." Louise put the phone down.

Byron got up from the windowsill, replaced the receiver, and grinned.

Chapter 19

But good God, people don't do such things!

—Henrik Ibsen, *Hedda Gabler*

The next morning, Louise was issued with a reroute notice. Normally she would have driven down Constitution Avenue, but today, the whole area from the White House to the Capitol Building was off-limits. It had been announced that a Martian spaceship was going to land in the Mall—at 11 A.M. All of the newspapers were full of it. MARTIANS TO ADDRESS CONGRESS! blared the headlines.

As early as 6:30 A.M., a special squad of Marine sharpshooters had been detailed to "pick off" all the birds in the area. By 9 A.M., police were patrolling the barriers and instructing everyone not to bring any birds and not to applaud when the Martians arrived.

As a sop to General Decker's demands, President Dale had allowed him to command a small force, but he was ordered to keep them well behind the barriers. By 9:15, he had deployed two dozen tanks around the area, and positioned platoons at vantage points on 17th Street, Independence Avenue, Pennsylvania Avenue, and around the White House and the Capitol.

In a special briefing, prior to this, Decker had explained to the platoon commanders that you could kill a Martian by shooting it in the head, and that, although he had been ordered to tell them to consider this a purely ceremonial job, to be prepared to engage. In fact, Decker got carried away and began improvising plans for capturing the spaceship, but he was interrupted by his second-in-command, Major General Runnells, who reminded him that this was beyond the scope of their orders.

By 10:45 A.M., the barriers were crowded with eager spectators and the usual news crews. Specially drafted meter maids walked among the crowds, holding placards stating: NO APPLAUSE! and NO BIRDS! Everyone was staring up at the sky, hoping to be the first to spot the flying saucer.

By 11 A.M., the House of Representatives was almost full. Every congressman and senator who

could make it was there. No one wanted to miss this one. Politicians, in their best suits, talked to friends and enemies alike, overcoming old enmities, making new rapprochements—inspired by the atmosphere of excitement. The astounding historical importance of this event made them forget they were really only brokers for businessmen. They began to feel like idealists, leaders, statesmen, men of destiny. It was an exhilarating sensation.

At the back of the podium, Donald Kessler, the man-who-was-everywhere, was supervising the installation of the translating computer. Professor Donald Kessler had left the alien autopsy in other qualified hands, and had rushed over to the Capitol.

Far away, across 17th Street, in Constitution Gardens, General Decker stood in his jeep, being driven past a row of tanks. He stopped to talk to the colonel commanding.

"How come we can't get any closer?" asked the colonel.

"Because my goddamn hands are tied," said Decker. "Just keep everybody on alert."

Suddenly, there was a swishing noise above them and they looked up. It was a flying saucer—coming in fast.

Behind the barriers around the Mall, the

crowds were thrilled. Some people started to clap, then remembered they shouldn't.

The flying saucer hovered for a moment, then descended, making a perfect landing on the grass outside the Capitol.

Dennis Veal, the Vice-President of the United States, hurried over to the spaceship, followed by the hand-picked reception committee. All eyes were on the spaceship. The time was 11:09 A.M.

The doorway opened and the ramp arched out, gleaming silver in the weak sunlight. The Martian ambassador appeared, followed by twelve domed Martian guards. They marched down the ramp.

They were met, on the grass, by the Vice-President who bowed and drew a circle in the air. This gesture was returned by the ambassador. Then, using sign language, Vice-President Veal ushered the visitors across the road and up the steps into the Capitol.

At the barriers, the crowds gazed in amazement, and TV cameras filmed it for the world.

In the main hall of Congress, on the podium, Chet Bickford, the ancient Speaker of the House, was addressing the assembled throng. Many of the congressmen weren't listening, absorbed in their own, urgent conversations. "This is a proud day for all Americans—and especially for

my good friends in Tennessee's Fifth District,"
intoned Bickford.

At the main doorway, a senator waved. This
meant the Martians had arrived.

Chet nodded and held up his hands. "Now,
if everybody would quiet down. I believe we're
ready. The Martian ambassador is here."

In the Oval Office, President Dale, the First
Lady, Taffy, and Jerry Ross watched the live TV
broadcast. The President looked at Jerry. "This
is a hell of a photo op. Are you sure I shouldn't
be there?"

"Ehh, for some picky reason, the Secret Service don't want the Executive Branch and the
Legislative Branch in the same place at the same
time," said Jerry.

The President nodded, and returned sadly to
the television.

In the main hall of Congress, the Martian ambassador came through the doorway, and the
hubbub from the senators and congressmen
died down. "Come on up here, Mr. Ambassador," boomed Bickford, in warm Southern
tones.

Filmed by a bank of TV cameras, the horrible-
looking Martian strode down the aisle, his shiny
cloak flowing behind him, followed by his
guards. Nothing so incongruous had been seen
in this historic hall since the visit of Red Cloud,

chief of the Sioux Indians, in 1870. The People's Representatives waited with bated breath.

"Welcome to Washington," said Chet Bickford, as the ambassador reached the podium.

The Martian ambassador stepped up.

"The Martian ambassador is going to say a few words," said Bickford and moved back, giving him space in front of the microphone.

Bickford joined Kessler at the rear of the stage, next to the translating computer and the technicians. Kessler's eyes glittered. He was deeply excited.

The Martian ambassador tapped the microphone. The technicians pressed the "record" button on the translating computer. Not a sound was heard in the crowded hall. The Martian ambassador tapped the microphone again. Then he reached under his cloak. Some of the congressmen quailed. Was he reaching for a gun? But no, of course not. The Martian ambassador pulled out a scroll on which was written his speech.

The congressmen relaxed and waited to hear what the skeleton-man from Mars was going to say. How was he going to explain the Pahrump Massacre? What were his concerns? Why was the Martian fleet in orbit around the Earth? There were so many questions that needed answers.

Before he spoke, the ambassador looked

around at the twelve Martian guards who were now standing in a line behind him. As he turned back to face Congress, he whipped out a raygun! The Martian guards also pulled out their weapons . . . and opened fire!

The first to go down was Dennis Veal, a great career cut tragically short, then Chet Bickford was dissolved, then, entire rows of congressmen. Politicians, leaping from their seats, were reduced to bones in an instant.

Screaming, running for the exits, cowering behind seats—the rayguns rained death upon all. There was no escape. Senators, congressmen, TV people, all were slaughtered. It was wholesale mass homicide. Bodies piled upon bodies, many of them with less flesh on them than a ham bone. The only good thing you could say about it was, it was fast.

In total shock, Donald Kessler ran up to the Martian ambassador.

"Mr. Ambassador, please!" he pleaded. "What are you doing? This isn't logical! This doesn't make sense!"

Whap! A Martian clubbed Kessler on the head. Donald had never felt anything so hard in his life, and was about to say something when he felt another blow penetrate his skull, a tidal wave of nausea, and he blacked out.

In less than a minute Congress had been

changed from the Western world's most elegant and sacrosanct assembly hall into a smashed-up, steaming slaughterhouse.

In the Oval Office, everyone stared at the carnage on TV.

"Not again!" groaned the President.

The First Lady sat rigid in her chair like a wax dummy.

Taffy, her face white, shifted on the sofa. "I guess it wasn't the dove," she said.

In the Anubis Lounge, surrounded by patrons of the Luxor, Barbara Land made a decision. Everyone around her was stunned by the massacre of Congress, but she knew what she had to do.

Far away, in the Midwest, at the Nightingale Retirement Home, Grandma and a group of old people were in the lobby watching television. They were perplexed. What were they watching? Was it a movie? Grandma decided it must be a comedy.

"They blew up Congress!" she exclaimed, and burst out laughing.

"Least now we won't have gridlock," quipped an old wag.

Next to Grandma sat the oldest man at the

home. His name was Herbert Everson and he was a hundred and two. He struggled forward in his chair, a look of anxiety in his rheumy eyes. "What happened to *Baywatch*?" he bleated.

In Washington, the Martians hurried down the Capitol steps—four of them carrying the unconscious Professor Kessler.

Half a mile away, in Constitution Gardens, General Decker shouted orders into his radio. "Get in there! Get in there and take them out!"

Four platoons converged upon the aliens, who had almost reached their spaceship. The soldiers were apprehensive, with good reason. They had seen the nightmarish things the Martian weapons could do.

Watching through binoculars, General Decker was fit-to-burst. He yelled into his radio: "Open fire! Open fire, Goddammit! What the Sam Hell are you waitin' for? Fire! Fire!"

As the Martians went up the ramp, the soldiers started shooting. The Martians swiftly combusted the platoons with raygun blasts, reducing most of the nearest troops to smoking bones. Behind the barriers, the spectators ran for their lives, or cowered on the ground, not daring to look up.

The little green men entered their spaceship, the ramp retracted, the door slid shut. . . .

Decker ordered the tanks to fire. A barrage of shells hit the spaceship and exploded. The whole area became a mass of dense black smoke. "We got 'em!" whooped General Decker. But then his face fell.

The flying saucer slowly ascended through the smoke. The cannon shells had had no effect at all!

For a moment, the spaceship hovered, and the air was filled with a nauseating high-pitched whine. Then it zoomed straight up.

General Decker shook his fists. "And stay out!" he yelled.

In Perkinsville, Kansas, at the back of Bob's Donuts, Richie and his coworker, Maria, gawked at the TV. Richie scratched his head. "What did they do that for?" he asked.

Maria took a sip of coffee. "Maybe they don' like the Earth peoples?" she said.

Chapter 20

In the arts of peace Man is a bungler.

—George Bernard Shaw

Three stories beneath the White House is a top-secret chamber that few people know about. It was built on orders from President Ronald Reagan. The story goes that, after his inauguration, Reagan was given a complete tour of the White House. At the end of the tour, he asked: "Where's the War Room?"

When he was informed there was no such thing, he was vexed. Ronald Reagan, not only an ex-movie star and ex-governor of California but also an ex-president of the Screen Actors' Guild, had thought the War Room in the film *Dr. Strangelove* was real.

One of his first acts as President was to demand that a War Room be built. The result was

a vast circular hall, with giant maps of the world
on the walls. These maps had imbedded cir-
cuitry, connected to computers, which permit-
ted them to convey sophisticated information.
Elegant curving bleachers lined the lower part
of the walls, reminiscent of the ancient Roman
Senate. Here, built-in work surfaces were laden
with state-of-the-art communications systems,
including satellite hookups and two-way video
phones.

In the center of the War Room, built into the
floor, was an enormous map of the world, also
fed electronically. The President's high-tech
desk was in the most commanding position, at
the apex of the bleacher-circle. Concealed lighting created a cathedral-like atmosphere, designed to reduce stress.

The room was now a mass of activity. Offi-
cials were running around like ants in a broken-
into anthill. Phones rang constantly, dealt with
by personnel seated high up in the bleachers.
Lower down, near the floor, were the seats occu-
pied by the Secretary of Defense, the Secretary
of State, General Decker, Jerry Ross, the joint
Chiefs of the Army, Navy, Air Force, Marines,
cabinet members, and intelligence officers.

On the floor, tactical staff were pushing de-
ployment symbols around the lit-from-beneath

world floor map. On the north wall, on the huge electronic world chart, clusters of pin spots displayed the strength, status, and positions of missile bases, armies, naval and submarine fleets, air defenses, and other military assets.

The President charged through the entrance door, which was ten inches thick and made of high-tensile steel, and hurried to his desk.

"Hello, gentlemen. Thank you for coming at such short notice." He turned to Decker, who was standing at his right, holding a clipboard. "It seems I owe you an apology, General."

"We all make mistakes, Mr. President," he said, with false humility.

"Well, not anymore!" Dale banged his fist on his desk. "We're gonna take charge of this thing!"

"Excellent!" said Decker, and moved toward him. "I've prepared the order." He handed Dale a clipboard on which was a piece of Pentagon stationery containing a neatly typed text.

"What's this?"

"Your executive order authorizing full use of our nuclear capability," said Decker. He handed him a pen. "You sign here, sir, at the bottom."

Dale stared at him. Nuclear weapons were a *deterrent*—you couldn't *use* them. To use nuclear weapons was to commit suicide because of

radioactive fallout. Didn't Decker know about fallout? Radioactivity kills almost everything. Only a few insect species were known to be able to survive high levels of radiation.

"Are you out of your mind? I'm not gonna start a nuclear war!" said Dale. Decker suppressed a sudden desire to strike the President in the face.

"With all due respect, sir, the war's already started! We gotta nuke 'em! We gotta nuke 'em now!"

The President could feel the pressure building inside his head like a tumor. He had always suspected Decker was psychotic, but, so far, he'd let it pass. After all, if psychosis were grounds for dismissal half the cabinet would have to go. "General Decker?" said the President.

"Yessir?"

"If you don't shut up, I will relieve you of your command."

Decker gasped. "But, sir, if we don't retaliate hard . . ."

"Shut up!" yelled the President. "Shut up! Shut up! *Shut up!*"

Decker lifted his clipboard delicately from the desk, like a rejected love note, and withdrew to his seat in the bleachers.

Dale rose, his expression grim. "Now, listen," he said firmly, to the faces watching him.

"We've got to let the people know they still have two out of three branches of government working for them. That ain't bad!" He looked around for confirmation. Some of the heads nodded. "I want people to know the schools are still open," he shouted. "I want people to know the garbage still gets picked up. I want a cop on every corner!" He turned abruptly to Jerry Ross. "How soon can we go on air?"

Jerry was taken unawares. He looked at his watch. "Uh . . ."

Two hours later, the President was doing what he did best—performing a speech to the nation. He gazed into the camera, sorrowful and sincere. "My fellow Americans, it is with a heavy heart that I speak to you this afternoon . . ."

Jerry Ross marveled at his boss's skill in making it look like he wasn't reading the Tele-PrompTer.

In Las Vegas, Barbara was in her kitchen listening to the President's speech on the radio.

"As you know," Dale said, "earlier today, the Martian ambassador and his cronies attacked and killed many of your representatives on Capitol Hill . . ."

Barbara was busy packing two suitcases and a large backpack with food and supplies.

In Washington, at Martin Luther King High, Annette Jones, an English teacher, had decided her class should watch the President's address on TV. There were twenty-eight fourteen-year-olds in her class, most of them black, and a few Hispanics.

Cedric Williams sat two desks from the front, next to the girl he loved. Her name was Alicia and she was so pretty he could only look at her for short bursts. Alicia was watching the President on TV.

"We opened our hearts and minds to our Martian neighbors, and this is how they have repaid us! The time for dialogue is over. I have decided to take the grave step of"—Dale paused dramatically—"*suspending diplomatic relations!*"

Alicia nodded. "That'll show them for blowing up Commerce!"

Cedric looked at her. "Not 'Commerce,'" he said. "Congress."

"Yeah, that's what I meant, Congress." She smiled at him and his heart turned over.

Three hundred miles due up, in the Martian flagship, the Martian leader and his lieutenants were watching their version of a TV—a giant globe resembling a crystal ball.

"I will be conferring with other world leaders

as time goes on," the President was saying. "Rest assured that, working together, we will soon come out at a very real outcome. Thank you."

The President faded out, to be replaced by the image of the presidential seal. The Martians reacted with great consternation. This was probably because of the American eagle depicted in the center of the presidential seal. Martians were oddly terrified of birds.

At one end of the colossal specimen hall, in the Martian operating theater, a group of small, green, megacephalic scientists were working on two experiments.

On one slab was Professor Kessler, completely dissected, but with all his separated body parts kept alive via tubes connected to a life-support machine. And on another slab was Nathalie's head, now sutured to the body of her chihuahua.

Kessler's head painfully opened its eyes. "Nathalie?" His voice sounded strange, paper-thin. "Nathalie, is that you?"

Nathalie's eyes opened at the sound of his voice. "Hi, Donald!" She tried to lift her head. But it was too heavy. "How are you feeling?" she said.

"Not terribly good, I'm afraid." He tried to

smile but the muscles in his face weren't working.

"Can I ask you something?" Nathalie's voice was full of short breaths, and she seemed to have acquired some of the eager personality of her dog.

"Yes, of course," replied Kessler, with some difficulty.

"Were you flirting with me on the show?"

Donald gazed at her face and tried to think. His mind was an unaccustomed blank.

"Because, if you were, I just want you to know, I liked it." Her pretty, cupid's-bow lips curled in a smile.

Without warning, Kessler's brain began to work. In a millisecond, he perceived everything. He perceived that he loved Nathalie. He perceived that love was completely in the mind. He perceived that love, held in the brain like water in a sponge, was the distinguishing characteristic of the human species. He perceived that love did not defy all scientific laws, as he had previously supposed; but that all scientific laws were a product of love. The question was moot as to where love came from because the fact of its existence was enough. Love defined itself. Like theological definitions of God, love was a prime mover. In a flash, he understood what Jesus meant when He said, "God is love."

"Yes," said Donald. "I *was* flirting with you. I couldn't help it. I think you're absolutely wonderful, Nathalie. In fact, I'm in love with you."

Nathalie grinned and wagged her tail.

Chapter 21

Things base and vile, holding no quantity,
Love can transpose to form and dignity.
Love looks not with the eyes, but with the mind,
And therefore is winged Cupid painted blind.

—William Shakespeare, *A Midsummer Night's Dream*

It was midnight in Washington, and Jerry Ross came out of the White House carrying his briefcase. He was exhausted. What a day!

He'd been up at the crack of dawn, preparing the news media for the Martians' address to Congress, and, of course, holding the President's hand. Then the Martians annihilated Congress, and he had to deal with the aftereffects, and, of course, hold the President's hand. *And*, he'd had to write the President's speech to the nation, *and* coach him through it, *and* congratulate him when it was done. And right after that, he went into a press conference.

It wasn't until nine p.m. that he realized he hadn't eaten all day. He ran down to the Secret Service kitchen and stole half a pastrami sandwich and a couple of Twinkies from the fridge. But he wasn't really hungry. When you're running on adrenaline, you lose your appetite. He didn't want food, what he really wanted was sex.

Scientists claim men think about sex every twenty minutes. Jerry thought that was a conservative estimate. He thought about it all the time. If he was angry, sex was the answer. If he was sad, sex was the solution. Whatever mood he was in, sex seemed to be the right thing to do.

He was once told, by a palm reader in the East Village, that he had an overactive libido. He thought about this and decided she was right.

For the next three years he went to an expensive psychiatrist. Then, one day, he came to the exhilarating realization that sex was absolutely fine! Some people liked fishing, some people liked to play golf, but, in his case, he liked sex. There was no need to feel bad about it, any more than you'd feel bad about sailing or skeet shooting. Sex was a healthy hobby undertaken for pleasure. What could be wrong with that? Life was for living, right? Have fun while you can, right? You only live once, right? And even if you live more than once, what's the difference?

Jerry crossed the White House parking lot to the limo. The driver was already at the passenger door. "Good evening, sir." He opened the door.

"Good evening, George." Jerry was about to step in when he noticed the girl. She stood alone, outside the White House gates, as if waiting for something to happen. Jerry froze. She was absolutely gorgeous! "Can you wait a second?" he said to the driver, and strolled across to the gates.

Her hair was coifed into an elaborate beehive. Her dress was made of some new translucent fabric, printed with delicate reddish-pink swirling patterns. It was form-fitting, right down to the ankles, but the material was so yielding you could see every contour of her body—and what a body! Jerry had never seen such breasts. They were like torpedoes. And what a slender waist! And what a perfect ass! She was so shapely! Everything on this girl was curved. Everything sang out: "Va Va Voom!"

"Excuse me, can I help you?"

The girl made eye contact and smiled. Her red lips seemed to be lit from within. Must be some new kind of lipstick, he thought.

"Are you interested in the White House?"

The girl batted her eyes.

Jerry wasn't sure about her eye makeup. It

was like a drag queen's, but she was no man—
not with that voluptuous figure!

"I work here. I'm the press secretary. Maybe
you've heard of me? My name's Jerry Ross."

The girl with the beehive hairdo stared at him
unblinkingly. He noticed she was chewing gum.

"Hey, are you doing anything? Do you want
to come in? I could give you a personalized tour.
Would you like that? The White House is quite
enchanting after hours."

The girl nodded. Jerry opened the gate and
she stepped through. "It's good to meet a new
face. You wouldn't believe the pressure of my
job." Jerry signaled to the driver to wait, took
her arm, and walked her across the parking lot
toward the White House. She was wearing an
intoxicating perfume, like musky peach, and
Jerry assessed that she was foreign—Swiss, or
maybe Czech.

They stepped up into the shadows of the Col-
onnade and he rapped on the French doors. On
the other side, Mitch, the young, buff Secret Service man, looked at them suspiciously.

"Hey, it's me. Can you let us in?"

Mitch unlocked the door. "I'm sorry, Mr.
Ross. We're just a little nervous here after what
happened to Congress."

"That's okay," Jerry said and led the girl
through.

"I'm just gonna give my friend here a little tour."

Mitch looked at the "friend." She was awesome. Where did Jerry find these girls?

Jerry led the girl down the corridor and into the main foyer. There was no one around. This was because President Dale was an early riser—in bed by eleven and up at six. This imposed a schedule on the White House. By this hour, midnight, everyone was in bed, except for staff security.

Jerry led the girl down the West corridor, and into the Hall of the Presidents. "Many great men and women have passed through here," he told her, in a hushed voice. "And now, *we're* passing through here. Feels good, don't it?" The girl was walking slightly behind him. There was something strange about the way she moved. Most people lead with their feet, but she was leading with her knees, as if she were skiing.

Jerry talked on, pointing out items of interest and giving his opinion of the various Presidents pictured in the portraits on the walls. The girl touched her right hand, which bore a large moonstone ring. A strange thing happened. The moonstone was really a kind of eyelid. It opened and an eye, on a stalk, came out of the ring and looked around. What the eye saw was transmitted to the Martian flagship.

In the command chamber of the Martian flag-ship, the Martian leader, flanked by four lieu-tenants, watched a large globe monitor. On it was a fish-eye view of the Hall of Presidents.

Jerry turned to the girl, and the eye retracted into the ring, closing its moonstone lid. "You're very graceful. What's your name?"

The girl smiled mysteriously.

"Do you speak English?"

The girl tilted her head.

"Ah, I see. So, where are you from?"

The girl shrugged.

"I know! Sweden, right? Sweden, am I right?"

The girl nodded.

"I knew it! All the most beautiful girls come from Sweden." He smiled, but she responded only with a blank stare, and didn't stop chewing her gum. Jerry thought he'd struck out, and turned to one of the portraits. "Ah, see that one? That's Thomas Jefferson—he wrote the Consti-tution. And this, of course"—he pointed to the next painting—"is George Washington. He never told a lie."

They strolled down to the end of the hall and turned a corner. Jerry stopped at an open door-way. "See this room? This is called the Roosevelt Room. This is where they sometimes have State banquets. It's a nice room, don't you think?"

The girl chewed her gum.

"The king of Sweden came here once, I believe," said Jerry, trying to impress.

There was a noise behind them. Taffy was on the North staircase, looking down at them, spooning jamocha almond fudge ice cream from a carton. "Ah, the midnight tour," she said. "Make sure he wears a condom!" She gave a mirthless smile and headed up the stairs. Jerry quickly took the girl's arm.

"Man, it sure is busy out here! Tell you what, there's a quieter room that is secret. The public doesn't know about it. You wanna see it?"

The girl with the fantastic beehive and even more fantastic breasts was chewing her gum hard, which made it appear as if she were nodding.

"Good," said Jerry.

He led her down a small hallway, at the end of which, on a plinth, stood a marble head of John F. Kennedy. Jerry put his hand on Kennedy's nose, and pushed. The head opened back on a hinge, revealing a small gray button. He smiled at his date and pressed the button. There was a muffled *clunk* and a section of wall slid open. Jerry lowered the Kennedy head back on its neck, took the girl's hand, and led her through. The wall closed behind them.

Jerry turned on the lights. The room was

round, with a sunken area in the center, containing a sumptuous round bed. The circular walls were adorned with fine murals depicting Hellenic nymphs and satyrs sporting and lovemaking in classical woods.

"We call this the Kennedy Room," he said.

The girl stopped to look at an immense glass fish tank, like a fairy kingdom filled with exotic tropical fish. On the other side of the tank, Jerry bent his knees and looked through the glass and the water and the swaying seaweed and the darting, gliding fish. Their eyes met. Jerry felt his manhood stirring. "Like it?"

He straightened up. She straightened up, too.

"Watch this." Jerry went to the bookcase, pulled out a copy of *How to Make a Perfect Martini* and the bookcase revolved into the wall, revealing a fully stocked bar. "Pretty nifty, huh? So, what'll you have?"

The calendar girl with the massive beehive hairdo watched Jerry carefully. "How about a Brandy Alexander?" He rubbed his hands together and grinned. "I guarantee you'll like it. I was a bartender in college!"

The girl ran her hands sensuously up and down her body.

"Wow, you're hot! But don't distract me, I gotta fix the drinks!" Jerry was thinking things

were working out great. He began humming to himself.

The girl swayed around the room. She stopped at a bronze statuette of a naked woman, and studied it. She stood back and compared her body with the body of the statuette. Then she undid the top three buttons of her dress. Jerry finished stirring the cocktails and glanced around.

"Ah, getting comfortable I see. That's good!"

She stepped down into the sunken area and sat on the bed. Jerry followed her down and gave her her glass. She took it, then took his drink, too. She put both drinks on the floor, pulled him toward her, and thrust her lips on his. They fell on the bed. She ripped open his shirt and bit him on the cheek.

"Ow!" he said, jerking up. "You're rough!" He smiled coyly. "But I like that!"

She arranged herself in a seductive pose and looked up at him, her eyes filled with promise. Jerry could not believe his luck.

"Whew! You're terrific!" he panted, and whipped off his tie and his shirt. Everything was perfect, except for one minor detail. The girl was still chewing her gum.

"Hey, baby, could you get rid of that gum?"

She didn't respond, so he gently put his finger into her mouth. "Here, let me do it."

She willingly opened her mouth wide. Then bit down hard! Her bite was so powerful, her teeth cut right through to the bone! The pain was excruciating! Jerry screamed! He tried to pull his finger out, but she had a jaw like a steel trap. He could feel, and hear, his finger bone breaking.

"Let go! Let go!" With his other hand, he tried to prise open her mouth. But, with a snap of her neck, she jerked back her head, ripping off his finger!

Aghast, Jerry looked down at his hands. His left hand was holding a piece of her lip and cheek. His right hand was missing its index finger. Blood squirted out of the stump.

Jerry hurled himself across the room to the phone, knocked the receiver off the hook and, with his good hand, punched out a number.

Behind him, the girl stepped out of the sin-pit and crossed to the aquarium where she spat out Jerry's finger, which floated down through the water and settled on the gravel floor. Blood seeped up in wispy trails, attracting the tenants of the tank. Soon the finger was lunch for a host of nibbling fish. "Hello! Hello! Operator! This is an emergency!" yelled Jerry into the phone. The girl picked up the bronze statuette, and whacked Jerry on the head. He was dead before he hit the floor.

The girl was taking lots of quick, shallow breaths and her face—with a gash in the right side of it revealing a hideous skeletal jawbone— was turning blue. She dropped the bloodied statuette and desperately looked for her purse. It was on the bed. She grabbed it and frantically snatched out a stick of gum. She tore off the gum wrapper and popped it into her mouth. Chewing rapidly, eyes closed, she sat on the edge of the bed, and, slowly, her breathing returned to normal.

After a few moments, she stood up, bent down and tore off the bottom of her dress. This dress had been hobbling her all evening. Now she could walk more easily.

She made her way to where they'd come in. There was a black button just below the light switch. She pushed it. She had guessed right. The wall slid open. She plucked a raygun from her purse and, with great care, peered out into the corridor. It was clear.

She stole silently around the corner to the North staircase and scuttled up the steps like a two-legged tarantula.

Earlier, at the briefing, she'd been made to memorize the layout of the White House. The target of her mission was on the third floor. To get there, she had to pass a security station. Her

superiors had formulated a plan to deal with this obstacle. She hoped the plan would work.

At the top of the stairs, she carefully turned the doorknob. She knew that on the other side of this door were the President's private living quarters. The door opened and she stepped into a thickly carpeted corridor. Halfway down was the security station. She could hear the low buzzing of a TV.

Covering the hole in her face with one hand, she stretched up to her full height and, remembering the catwalk footage she had studied during training, sashayed down the hall.

At the desk, leaning back in his chair, Jim Creed, the Secret Service man, was watching *Beavis and Butthead* on his portable Sony. It was the episode where Beavis and Butthead try to get drunk on nonalcoholic beer. Next to the TV were a bank of video monitors, on which, if he had been paying attention, he would have seen the Martian girl.

Suddenly he heard a cracking noise and a high-pitched female, "Oh!" He looked into the hall and saw what looked like a Vegas showgirl, bending over to take off her shoes. It appeared she had broken one of her heels. Jim Creed took off his dark glasses—the better to admire her shapely rear end. "Hey, lady, you're not sup-

posed to be here," he said, his tone official, but friendly.

The girl peered at him from under her armpit. Jim smiled. Quick as a flash, up came her raygun and Pzzzzzztt!! Jim was blown through the air. His body hit the ceiling and disintegrated.

The Martian girl watched the body fragments shower the floor and felt uncomfortable. This was bad. Now that she was so close to the fulfillment of her mission, she needed to feel comfortable and alert. Nothing could go wrong. She made a decision. The head—it was too restricting. It had to go.

She hunched her shoulders and gripped the top of her beehive. With a supreme effort, she tugged hard and pulled it off. The wig was sealed to her fake human face, so this came off, too, dragged slowly over her own real face, and splitting apart as she wrenched it over her massive brain. She tossed the loathed facade away, and felt much better.

The picture she now presented was incongruous in the extreme: the ideal female form, attired in a graceful couturier dress, with a gruesome bulging-brained Martian skull-face sticking out the top of it.

Not far away, in the President's bedroom, James Dale opened his eyes. Had he heard something? He looked around the dark room.

Marsha was beside him, her head in curlers, snoring gently. Rusty, the dog, was asleep on the floor beside her. All appeared to be well. The President fluffed up his pillow and sank back to sleep.

Softly, the bedroom door opened and the Martian girl stepped in. On her hand, the eye-on-a-stalk was looking at everything.

In the command chamber of the flagship, the Martian leader, together with his four lieutenants, watched their crystal ball-like monitor. It showed a fish-eye view of the President's bedroom.

The Martian leader noticed something moving in the distorted corner of the image. Suddenly, he jerked back. It was a dog! The dog was asleep but its nose quivered. The Martians all reacted with alarm. Martians had no fear of humans, but dogs were another story. Why were Martians petrified of dogs? Who knew?

In the President's bedroom, Dale's golden retriever, though asleep, smelled something bizarre. As the President's favorite pet, Rusty often traveled with him and was the envy of every dog he met. He was the canine equivalent of a billionaire because he had experienced an encyclopedic cornucopia of odors from all over the world. But he had never smelled anything like this before. His eyes popped open. What he

saw made the hair stand up on his back. It was a Martian with a DD-cup bosom pointing a gun at his master! His reaction was instantaneous.

The girl saw the dog coming at her out of the corner of her eye. She fired at the snarling fur-covered monster. Pzzzzzztt! With a piteous howl, Rusty was incinerated—converted to a pile of bones that dropped to the bedroom floor.

The President and the First Lady woke and Marsha screamed! The Martian girl fired. Pzzzz-zztt! The blast hit the bedspace between them.

Dale rolled out on the right side, Marsha the left. The Martian girl fired again, blowing a hole in the wall above the President's head. Terrified, the First Lady crouched below the bed. Her eye fell on Rusty's steaming skull.

President Dale cowered on all fours. There was no escape. The Martian girl took aim at his head.

"No! Please! Don't!" he begged.

Marsha seized Rusty's skull and pitched it, with all her might! Whap! It cracked the Martian girl on the head and she squeaked.

Then the bedroom door flew open revealing Mitch, his gun drawn. Behind him were three more men in suits with guns. The President jumped to his feet. The Martian girl swung behind him, grabbing him around the throat, and put her raygun to his head.

"Don't shoot!" hollered Mitch to the other Secret Service men.

The Martian pulled President Dale backward toward another doorway, and kicked it open. It was a large dressing room, lined with closets.

Keeping her eyes clamped on the men, the Martian girl didn't notice a tall, freestanding Victorian birdcage, covered with a cloth. She bumped into it. The cage wobbled, the cloth slipped, and a startled parakeet screeched! The Martian girl spun and fired. Pzzzzzztt! The parakeet exploded!

"Get down!" bellowed Mitch, and fired.

His bullet drilled straight into the Martian girl's brain! Brain-gunk spurted in all directions, and she thumped to the floor, pulling the President with her. Dale, covered in slime and brain-gook, slowly got up.

"Thanks, Mitch."

Mitch gave the briefest of nods. "It's my job," he said.

The Martian leader hated failure. He turned from the globe monitor, slapped one of his lieutenants in the face, and, mad as a hornet, spat out a barrage of orders. The whole control chamber was instantly galvanized. Gesticulating wildly, they hissed and squawked into their instruments.

The leader hoisted himself onto his throne and pulled a lever. The throne rose straight up on its silver pole. A hatchway opened in the ceiling and the throne, and the leader vanished through it.

A loud siren wailed. It could be heard in all the beehive chambers of the ship. One floor below, a thousand Martians climbed into their battle suits. In the armory, they queued for weapons and ammunition. In the hold, a hundred giant robots, made of the hardest Martian metal and as high as a house, stepped out of their pods.

A door opened in the top of each robot's bubblehead and, from a hanging gantry, the Martian robo-operators slid down chutes into the heads.

Upstairs in the specimen chamber, Nathalie and Kessler had been placed next to each other on a display shelf. She was still half-chihuahua and he was still surrounded by his own limbs and organs. The noise of the siren was making Nathalie nauseous. They watched fifty Martians march past, all carrying Martian flags.

"What's happening?" said Nathalie.

"I don't know!" the great scholar lamented. "I don't know anything anymore!" Donald had never felt so frustrated in all his life.

Nathalie, overflowing with love and sympa-

thy, observed his wonderful face. Poor Donald! How hard it was for him to adjust to being only a head!

"Oh, Nathalie," he moaned, gazing into her warm, blue eyes. "If only I could hold you in my arms!"

The noises in the ship increased. Mingling with the brain-splitting clamor of the siren, came strange electrical whirring sounds—what were they?—and the staccato bursts of rayguns being test-fired, and the deep throbbing of the giant robots' engines.

"Oh, Donald," whimpered Nathalie. "I'm scared!"

Out in Space, the Martian fleet was on the move. One by one, they broke out of orbit and began to descend.

The first flying saucers pierced the ionosphere, their spinning silver rims sending out sparks of green light. They were followed by the second wave. The third wave formed up behind them—and behind them, the fourth, the fifth, and the sixth.

Silver wave followed silver wave, swooping down through the Earth's atmosphere toward the distant blue-green surface. The Martian attack had begun!

Chapter 22

Who knows but the world may end tonight?

—Robert Browning

In the laboratory of the Ross Perot Annex of the Science Building, at Georgetown University, three doctors and a nurse were doing an autopsy on the Martian girl assassin.

There was a knock. Framed in the small glass window in the door, was the face of the lab technician who'd gone to get an analysis of the blue gumlike substance found in the Martian's mouth. The nurse let him in. The three doctors looked at him with interest.

"So," said the first doctor. "Do we know what it is?"

"It's NO_2—very highly concentrated."

"Nitrogen!" exclaimed the second doctor.

"Of course!" cried the third doctor. "That's how it could breathe in our atmosphere!"

The nurse heard a spooky swishing noise. "What's that?" she queried.

The others heard it, too. It sounded like a vast flock of birds—no, more like the wind blowing in a forest of trees, no . . . whatever it sounded like, it affected them all the same way. It was creepy. They looked out the window.

"Oh my God!" said the first doctor.

"I don't believe it!" said the second doctor.

Throughout Washington, D.C., in the streets, the offices, the stores, the factories, the parking lots, the gas stations, the parks, the schools, the golf courses, in fact, everywhere where humanity gathered, people stared at the sky.

In the Oval Office, the First Family was having tea with the Dalai Lama. "More tea, Dalai?" said Marsha, teapot in hand.

"Yes, thank you. This is very nice tea."

"It's Jasmine," said Taffy, trying to be well-behaved.

"So, how do you like Washington?" inquired Dale. "I guess it's a little different from Tibet, huh?"

"Yes, it is," concurred the Dalai Lama. "For example, we don't have these flying objects. What do you call them?"

"Flying objects?" frowned Dale.

The Dalai Lama pointed out the window. "Those."

The First Family turned in their seats and looked out the window. The sky was filled with spaceships—and they were coming down fast!

Mitch came in through the door, his face white. "It's a full-scale invasion! Come on! We need to get you to safety!"

They got up and hurried out into the corridor, which was full of Secret Service men, talking into their radios.

The President, the First Lady, Taffy, and the Dalai Lama followed Mitch past the security station and into the Hall of Presidents.

"Where are we going?" panted the President.

"The War Room!" shouted Mitch. "Come on!"

"Shouldn't we go that way?" said the First Lady, pointing.

"Sorry, ma'am," said Mitch. "There's a tour going through there."

"Oh."

In the next room, a school tour was, indeed, in progress. The female tour guide, a thin woman in a turquoise suit, was addressing a group of twenty high school students, which included Cedric and Neville.

"The Blue Room," announced the tour guide, "is often considered the most beautiful room in

the White House. In fact, it is often used by the President to receive guests."

From above, came the sound of something crashing.

"What's that?" said Cedric.

"It is furnished to represent the period of James Monroe." She was standing beside a painting of an eighteenth-century gentleman.

There was another, heavier crash.

"What's that?" said Neville.

"That is a portrait of James Monroe," said the tour guide, pleased that one of the kids had finally asked a question.

The students looked terrified and began moving backward. What are they doing now? thought the tour guide, not seeing the Martian behind her. Pzzzzzztt! She was charred to the bone.

The students screamed and ran. Cedric and Neville dropped behind a sofa. Two Secret Service men burst through the doorway, firing! The Martian dodged, and bullets bounced off his body-armor. He shot a stream of high-intensity rays at the two men. They died quickly, burning to a crisp. A .38 Police Special fell near the sofa. Cedric grabbed it. The Martian advanced into the room. POW! Cedric shot him in the head. The Martian's glass dome shattered, his brain spewed gook, and he crumpled to the floor.

"Very cool," said Neville.

"No problem," said Cedric.

Neville picked up the other Secret Service man's gun.

The entire metropolis was in a panic. Flying saucers were landing all over the city, and disgorging Martian troops. At every intersection, cars and trucks were crashing into each other. People ran yowling through the streets, pursued by the merciless little green men from Mars.

A spaceship hovered above the White House. A cannon emerged from the undercarriage and spat a stream of fusion-energy at the roof. The entire top floor burst into fragments!

Inside the White House, all was confusion. Plaster fell from the ceilings, columns crashed, staircases and floors collapsed, and the halls were thick with smoke.

The presidential party had turned back from its original route because of a fallen wall.

"Keep moving, Mr. President! We have to get you to the back stairs!"

The President, the First Lady, and the Dalai Lama were covered in plaster dust.

"We lost Taffy!" cried Dale.

A Martian appeared through the smoke. Mitch dove in front of the President to protect him. Pzzzzzztt! The blast bit off part of his arm. Unfazed, he fired back. Pow! Pow! Pow! The

Martian lost his balance, shooting a long death-ray burst across the ceiling. A large chandelier broke loose.

"Oh no!" shouted the First Lady, in horror. "Not the Nancy Reagan chandelier!"

It tore from its moorings and plummeted straight down on top of her—crushing her flat.

Dale got up. "Marsha! Marsha?"

"Get down!" yelled Mitch, wounded.

The Martian aimed his raygun at the President and was about to fire when three bullets smashed into his dome. Brain bubbling, he dropped dead.

Cedric and Neville appeared, guns smoking. Mitch stared at them. Two black school children had just saved the President's life!

"What you gawkin' at?" shouted Cedric. "Get that President outta here!"

Suddenly, another Martian appeared. In one synchronized move, Cedric and Neville blasted him. The Martian's head blew off.

"Rush!" yelled Cedric.

"Gravity!" yelled Neville.

They slapped their hands together in a low-five.

Mitch and the President staggered out through a doorway. The Dalai Lama had mysteriously disappeared.

In the sky, a squadron of F-106 Delta Dagger jet fighters launched their missiles at the flying saucers below. None of the saucers, which were made of a metal harder than anything known on Earth, were even scratched.

From out of the clouds, a flock of saucers swooped down on the jets, pumping ring-fire. Three jets exploded in midair—two spun out of control. One, which flew low over the Capitol, was hit, lost a wing, and went into a spin—smashing into the National Museum of American History. Another fell like a stone into the Potomac. The others flew off at top speed, with saucers on their tails.

A Boy Scout troop stood at the base of the Washington Monument, watching the dogfights in the sky.

In one of the spaceships, two Martian pilots looked down. The first Martian pilot said something to the second, who grunted and punched a button. Boom! There was a flash of light and a high-energy beam smacked right into the base of the Monument. The Monument cracked and began to fall in the direction of the Boy Scouts. They turned and ran the other way.

In the flying saucer, the first pilot squealed, stomped on the foot pedal, and turned the wheel.

The Boy Scouts were out of danger. But then,

the saucer hopped over the falling Monument, caught it on its rim, and flipped it back over! The shadow of the Monument fell over the Boy Scouts. Some of them looked up and screamed. Then it landed with an earth-shattering crash and the Boy Scouts were no more.

Chapter 23

Old and young, we are all on our last cruise.

—Robert Louis Stevenson

Thirty flying saucers glided over the city of Las Vegas. One after the other, they flew in row formation, low above the Strip. Tourists and locals watched the parade in amazement. The spaceships circled around and flew back. This time, though, complicated patterns of constantly changing lights radiated from each one. The people in the streets gazed at the dazzling glory of the light show. It put the famous Vegas hotel signs to shame!

Above the intersection where the Strip and Flamingo Road meet, the saucers stopped dead and arranged themselves horizontally, one above the other, like a stack of pancakes. As word spread of the spaceship display, crowds poured from the casinos to watch.

"What is that?" asked a little girl of her father.

"They must be opening some new hotel."

The pancake stack of flying saucers rose in the air, then split off, one by one, each going in a different direction. On the streets below, the audience cheered and applauded.

The saucer's magic lights went out, but were replaced by the incandescence of raygun fire, decimating the crowds below. People screamed and ran for cover.

Two blocks from the Strip, in Art Land's sumptuous office in the soon-to-be-completed Galaxy Hotel, a buffet dinner had been prepared. Linen-covered tables, laden with goodies, were arranged against the walls. Tuxedoed waiters stood at attention, pretending not to watch the conference that was going on in the middle of the opulent office.

A group of financial investors sat around the large cedar table, listening to Art Land's presentation. In the middle of the table stood the scale model of the Galaxy Hotel and Casino.

Art, in his best rhinestone-studded suit, faced the investors, dramatically framed by the floor-to-ceiling windows behind him.

". . . and I guarantee your investment will be returned within the first five months of operation."

The investors were worried by the sounds

coming from outside. A Saudi Arabian prince, dressed in white robes, put up his hand.

"Excuse me please . . ."

Art waved him down. "Just a minute. Gambling is a leisure activity that will never go out of style! Look at the last few days—even in a time of national crisis, people still want to play blackjack!"

A tall, elderly Texan businessman half rose from his chair. "Mr. Land, I believe we oughtta reconvene this meeting at a later time . . ."

"Five more minutes! I want you to see our beautiful showroom! It's stupendous! And it's going to attract the biggest stars!" He pressed a catch, opening the hotel model, revealing a cross-section of the interiors, like a dollhouse. "I tell ya, the Galaxy Hotel is going to change the face of Vegas as we know it!"

Hands on hips, Art leaned back and nodded his head vigorously, like a chicken. "Am I worried about the competition? Hoo Boy! When the Galaxy opens, we're gonna blow those suckers away!"

A flying saucer appeared outside the window and fired! The plate-glass windows shattered. A hot, fiery wind blew through the room. Everything was swept before it—the model, the tables, the investors, the waiters . . . And Art's colossal blue and silver globe of the Earth broke

from its housing. The floor split, the walls caved in, and the giant globe rolled into Art, pushing him out through the space where the window had been. He plunged forty-four stories to the parking lot. Shortly afterward, the Galaxy Hotel and Casino collapsed.

Arthur Land and his dreams were as if they had never been.

In the Luxor, Byron was on the phone. He had just got through to his ex-wife.

"Louise? It's me. I've been trying to call you all day. The flight was canceled . . ."

There were weird noises coming down the phone.

"Hello? Hello? Louise? Are you there? I can't hear you."

In Washington, Cedric and Neville had fought their way home and were now protecting their mother. Cedric was stationed at one window, Neville at the other. On their journey home, they had acquired two automatic rifles. Louise was crouched behind the sofa, the phone to her ear. Loud sounds of battle came from outside.

"Byron, there's Martians everywhere!" she cried.

A nearby explosion rocked the room. The two boys ducked and the phone went dead.

In Las Vegas, Byron tried to get a line, but it was no use. He felt panic propagate inside him, but quashed it. He knew what he had to do. He had to get to Washington.

In another part of the casino, Dolores Snyder, the white-haired old lady with a passion for slots, was pumping nickels into two machines. Behind her, across the aisle, Joe Weinberg, the lawyer, was playing roulette. He noticed the big-chested Cindy go by with a tray of glasses.

"Hey," he yelled. "It's the end of the world—stop watering the drinks!"

Standing on the main staircase that led from the casino to the games floor, Larry Bava was making a speech to a crowd of anxious guests.

"Please everyone," he implored. "If we can just keep calm, we can get through this! The army's arrived and they will have the situation under control very soon. Until then, please stay inside, make use of the many excellent facilities of the hotel, and, once again, thank you for coming to the Luxor."

Byron went around to all the staff stations looking for a phone that worked. He heard someone call his name. It was Barbara Land.

"Byron! Do you know anyone who can fly a plane?"

"Yeah, your husband, Art."

"No, he's dead."

Byron blinked.

"I told him this was going to happen!" exclaimed Barbara. "I even loaded the plane with supplies!" She stared up at the ex-heavyweight champion of the world, her hair a mess and a dim sparkle of perspiration around her mouth. She looked like a crazy woman.

"I want to go to Tahoe. To the Tahoe caves! It's remote. The Martians won't find it!"

"Where's the plane?"

"Private airfield. On the other side of the freeway."

"Could it fly to Washington, D.C.?"

"Why?" Barbara shouted. "I want to go to Tahoe!"

Outside, flying saucers were strafing the city. But, in some places, people were still unaware of what was happening. For example, Tom Jones, the well-known singer, and his band, were performing to a packed house. They had reached the instrumental section of his hit song, "It's Not Unusual" and Tom was wowing the audience with his sexy dance moves.

Suddenly, two Martians walked onstage, and enthusiastically imitated his dance movements. The band came to a ragged halt and the audience bolted from their seats. Tom Jones turned, and the Martians, no more than six feet away, pulled out their rayguns.

"Good God!" said Tom.

The Martians opened fire. Rushing for the exits, the terrified theatergoers were massacred. Tom ran into the wings. One of the Martians fired at him, but hit the side of the proscenium.

Tom burst through some drapes into the backstage area. A troupe of showgirls were getting ready to go on.

"Girls! Get out! Get out! There's a Martian right behind me!"

The girls screamed and scattered. The Martian appeared and fired. Tom ducked through the stage door and ran down a short hallway, through a door, and into the casino, almost colliding with Byron and Barbara.

"There's a Martian right behind me!" he gasped.

Joe Weinberg rushed over. "Hey, you're Tom Jones! 'It Ain't Unusual'—right? Tom! I don't believe it! This is great! Anyone got a pen?"

Cindy passed by.

"How 'bout you? You got a pen?"

A death ray exploded through the door! Everyone ran, except Dolores Snyder. No way was she going to leave her slots. She'd been working them for two hours, and she knew they were getting ready to pay off.

The Martian came through the smoking doorway, saw the old lady, and took aim. Byron

sprang out and threw a hard right-cross into the Martian's dome. It smashed and the Martian screamed! His dome filled with green gas, and he fell, shrieking to the floor.

Tom Jones, Barbara, and Cindy came out from behind the slot machines, and watched him die.

"That was some punch," said Tom, putting out his hand. "I'm Tom Jones."

Byron gave his hand a quick shake. "Byron Williams."

"I saw you box once—in Cardiff, Wales."

"Uh-huh? Get his gun. You might need it."

"Okay."

Tom picked up the dead Martian's raygun. Byron took the ray pistol from the Martian's holster and glanced at Barbara. Blood was trickling down her head. "You okay, Barbara?"

She grinned bravely. "Yeah, just a scratch. What I need is a drink!"

"You and me both, baby," said Joe Weinberg, emerging from under the roulette table.

Tom Jones looked around urgently. "We've got to get out of here."

"Do you know how to fly a plane?" Byron asked him.

"Sure—you got one?"

Byron pointed to Barbara.

"She has."

Everyone looked at Barbara.

Outside, the spaceships had landed and off-loaded their troops. From Downtown to Circus Circus, the invaders roamed the streets, blowing away cars, buses, humans—anything that moved. People ran from the hotels, where they were sitting ducks, to take their chances on the street. Some were lured out by a Martian carrying a device that broadcast loudly, in English, the message: "We are your friends! We are your friends!"

Tanks and armored cars rolled down the Strip and met the Martian ground troops outside the Treasure Island Hotel.

In the artificial lake, the mock battle between a square-rigged British galleon and a pirate ship, was in progress. Both ships were blown to bits by Martian raygun blasts. The army tanks fared no better. Nothing could withstand the devastating power of the Martian weapons.

Chapter 24

"The gods are on the side of the stronger."

—Tacitus

Even the obscure and remote town of Perkinsville, Kansas, was not exempt from the Martian attack. At around lunchtime, a flying saucer was seen hovering over the town. Chucky, the "one big no-good vagrant bum," came into Bob's Donuts.

"Hey, Richie," he said, at the door. "Come take a look."

Richie ducked down through the gap under the counter, crossed the room, and followed him out.

On the street, people stared up at the miracle in the sky.

"Awesome!" gasped Richie.

"Yeah!" said Chucky.

They stood and gazed at the unearthly vision of the flying saucer. A hoselike tube emerged from beneath the saucer's rim. Pzzzzzztt! A stream of white flame blew up Bob's Donuts.

Richie turned pale.

"Lord!" exclaimed Chucky.

The saucer fired again. Boom! The gas station exploded! The people scattered. The saucer fired again and again, blowing up Ace Video Rentals and Judy's Ladieswear and—a massive explosion this—the oil storage depot.

Richie didn't know what he was doing, all he knew was he was running. He felt like a deer in the woods, pursued by hunters with telescopic rifles. He ran down this street and that, making himself a hard target. At the end of an alley he vaulted over the wall into the backyard of Dorothy's Hair Salon, hotfooted it across the yard, climbed over the opposite wall and dropped down into the parking lot across from the sheriff's office. Then he heard the swishing noise of the saucer above. *Boom!* Dorothy's Hair Salon erupted! The force of the explosion threw Richie off his feet, into the side of a police cruiser. It took him a moment to recover.

When he did, he saw the saucer pass overhead, its cannon aimed at the sheriff's office. He ducked. *Boom!* The sheriff's office was blown into a thousand fragments.

Richie picked himself up, noticed the keys were in the ignition of the dented cruiser, opened the door, slid behind the wheel, and started it up.

He drove like a demon through the burning streets of Perkinsville, dodging abandoned vehicles and panicking pedestrians. At the intersection of Hoover Street, a dog jumped in front of him. He swerved, rode up over the pavement, crashed through two parking meters, and slammed into the back of a burning bakery truck.

The flying saucer passed overhead. Richie knew he had to get out of the car fast. He threw himself out and sprinted, low, along the side of a warehouse building. *Boom!* Searing hot air punched the back of his head, and he was thrown to his knees.

Richie didn't look back. He got up and ran.

In the Norris trailer, a shrine had been erected to the memory of Billy-Glenn. One whole corner of the living area was filled with souvenirs: a large bronze bust of the hero, made and donated, free of charge, by a famous sculptor from Kansas City; the wreath given by the President of the United States, bearing the presidential seal, various other wreaths and artifacts, includ-

ing the prototype, from Mattel, of a Billy-Glenn doll.

The corner walls were a mass of newspaper and magazine clippings featuring the flag defender of Pahrump, and, in pride of place, in a gold frame, hung the now-famous Iwo Jima photograph.

Glenn Norris, who had put on his old 'Nam army fatigues, was greasing the chamber of his army-service revolver, and Sue-Ann was loading her shotgun.

Outside, the dog, Prince, was barking, and, in the distance, they could hear the sound of buildings exploding in Perkinsville. Glenn ground his teeth. The noises brought back sharply the nightmare of the Tet Offensive.

The door flew open and Richie ran in. "A flying saucer blew up the donut shop!"

"You're kiddin' me!" said Glenn.

Breathing hard, sweat and dirt running down his face, Richie put out his hand. "Give me the keys to the truck. I'm gonna get Grandma."

Glenn shook his head. "Forget Grandma, she's halfway to outer space already." Glenn held out the revolver. "Take this. The shells are in that box on the table."

Sue-Ann snapped her shotgun barrel shut. "I'll tell ya one thing, Richie," she said, her face determined. "They ain't gettin' the TV!"

In Washington, deep below the White House, the War Room was frantic. On the big wall maps, thousands of different-colored lights were blinking. The tiny green lights indicated Martian forces. U.S. forces were tiny red lights, Europeans were blue, Arabs were purple, Africans were orange, and Asians were yellow. Over every continent, the green lights spread as the others were extinguished.

The President sat at his desk, bewildered. "What happened to Marsha?" he cried. "Is she dead? Where's Taffy? And where's my dog?"

A voice said: "The president of France on line two!" But he didn't hear it. He couldn't hear the clamor of the men and women around him—orchestrating tactics, ordering troop movements, receiving and transmitting information to and from the many, constantly changing theaters of war. He couldn't hear anything.

"Where did I go wrong?" he mourned. "I should've stayed in local politics. I was happier back then."

"The president of France is on line two!"

Dale looked up. A military aide was talking to him.

"Line two, Mr. President."

Dale picked up the phone and punched a but-

ton. "Hello? Ah, hello Maurice! Comment ca va?"

In Paris, France, in a magnificent stateroom in the Élysée Palace, the French president stood at a large window, looking at the Eiffel Tower. "Ah, James, I 'ave good news for you. You will be pleased when I tell you this. The Martian ambassador, he is here—and we 'ave negotiated a settlement."

Sitting at a large conference table, crowded with French politicians, was the Martian ambassador and four Martian guards.

In the War Room, President Dale's mind quickly cleared. "Get out! Maurice! Get out of the room now!"

The sound of raygun blasts, human screams, and shattering glass came from the receiver. The President held the phone away from his ear and groaned.

In the stateroom, in the Élysée Palace, the Martians shredded the French cabinet. Outside the window a flying saucer fired and the Eiffel Tower fell!

In Perkinsville, in a mobile home, at the opposite end of the trailer park, a man and a woman were making love. Their bedroom was decorated like a '70s love nest, with lava lamps, fairy lights, and a disco ball. Looking at the two lov-

ers through the window, were two lascivious Martians.

As the passion of the lovers increased, the Martians' domes fogged up. The woman suddenly noticed the hideous Peeping Toms.

"Mike! Mike!" She pointed at the Martians. Small windshield wipers had appeared inside their domes. They were going at speed, wiping the glass clear!

In the Norris trailer, Richie, Glenn, and Sue-Ann heard the sound of raygun blasts.

"What was that?" said Sue-Ann.

She and Glenn looked out the window. The truck keys were hanging off a peg on the wall. Richie saw his opportunity and grabbed them. He went for the door.

"Hey! Where you going?" yelled Glenn.

"I'm gonna get Grandma."

"No you ain't," said Glenn. "You're gonna stay here and defend this trailer!"

"That's what Billy-Glenn would do!" accused Sue-Ann.

"You leave here, and you're disgracing an American hero!" bellowed Glenn.

"I don't care. I'm gonna get Grandma!" Richie yanked open the door.

"Richie!" yelled Sue-Ann. "You come back here!"

Richie ran to the pickup, jumped in, and drove away.

In the doorway, Glenn yelled curses at his son, trailing off when he became aware of a strange humming/crunching noise. He looked around, noticed that the dog, Prince, had slipped his collar and was nowhere around, and went back inside.

"What the hell is that noise?" he said to Sue-Ann.

"I don't rightly know!" she replied, scared.

A sixty-foot robot came through the trees and entered the trailer park. Inside its glass bubble-head, a Martian operated the controls.

The robot hooked the Norris trailer up in the air in its huge metal pincers. Inside, Glenn and Sue-Ann were hit by tumbling objects, as their home twisted upside-down. They slid and skidded down the walls, trying to grip on to things. Sue-Ann clung to the bathroom door handle, Glenn clung to the kitchen faucet. The bathroom door tore off and Sue-Ann plummeted into Glenn. He lost his hold on the faucet and crashed on top of the door, which was on top of his wife, and was struck in the head by the TV. Sue-Ann blacked out and the sofa rammed Glenn hard in the back. Before he had time to register his dislocated vertebrae, there was an explosion of stars! The giant robot had picked

up a second trailer, and was smashing them together! Glenn and Sue-Ann Norris were crushed
to a pulp.

Richie saw, in the rearview mirror, the giant
robot destroying the trailer park. Too shocked to
do anything but drive, he put the pedal to the
metal and accelerated down the highway.

In Washington, in the War Room, President Dale
was comatose with depression. General Decker
tried to get his attention. "Mr. President!"

Dale lifted his head off the desk. He looked
twenty years older than he had that morning.

"Mr. President!" Decker thrust a pen in his
hand. "You have to sign!"

"What is it?" said the President. "My last will
and testament?"

"No, sir, it's your order to deploy our nuclear
capability."

The President signed the paper.

Chapter 25

The time is out of joint; O cursed spite,
That ever I was born to set it right!

—William Shakespeare, *Hamlet*

In the Utah desert, a silo opened. There was a deep rumbling sound. The desert floor shuddered, and a nuclear missile shot out of the ground and into the sky. The Martian flagship, in space, was its target.

In the War Room, everyone watched the large satellite monitor on which the missile could be seen ascending through the layers of the Earth's atmosphere. The President's face was ashen.

Inside the command chamber of the Martian flagship, the leader and his lieutenants saw the incoming missile. The Martian leader waved his arms, yakking with alarm. The lieutenants acted quickly. They picked the Martian leader up off

his throne, and carried him across the room to an instrument panel. He bent down and pulled a lever.

Just below the rim of the flagship, a hatch opened and a party balloon floated out. But it was no ordinary party balloon. It had two antennae sticking out of it and a trumpetlike nozzle.

The nuclear missile was closing fast on the flagship. What happened next, happened in a matter of microseconds. The nose cone of the missile touched the fuselage of the spaceship. This sent a message to the ignition system, which initiated a thermonuclear reaction. At the same time, the nozzle on the balloon opened, sucked the explosion in, and expanded in size.

Inside the command chamber, shock waves knocked the Martians over. Outside, the now fat balloon floated back through the hatch.

In the War Room, everyone watched the screen, baffled.

"What happened?" said Decker.

In the Martian command chamber, a cadet came in, carrying the fat balloon. He marched up to the Martian leader, now back on his throne, and presented it to him. The Martian leader took the nozzle of the balloon into his mouth and inhaled. Then he spoke to his lieutenants, and his voice came out high and squeaky! The lieutenants fell about laughing!

In the War Room, all was quiet. Mitch, the Secret Service man, his arm in a sling, where he'd taken the raygun blast, stared at the unharmed spaceship on the screen.

"Only God can help us now," he muttered, under his breath.

Chapter 26

Believe me! The secret of reaping the
greatest fruitfulness and the greatest
enjoyment from life is to live dangerously!

—Friedrich Nietzsche

Six miles outside of Perkinsville, Richie's pickup
hauled-ass along the highway, chased by a giant
robot. Looking in the rearview mirror, there was
no doubt—the robot was gaining.

Despite all the work done by thinkers, philos-
ophers, playwrights, novelists, psychologists,
and journalists, human nature is not completely
explicable. Why is it that danger will cloud the
mind of one person, yet sharpen the wits of another? Grasping for some way to evade the
sprinting robot, Richie's eye fell upon a line of
pylon towers. Holding his breath, keeping the
gas pedal pressed to the floor, he jerked the
wheel to the right, and the truck flew off the

highway, and crashed through the wire fence.
Holding hard to the wheel, Richie bucked across
the uneven pasture, heading for the towers.

The giant robot came off the road after him,
and Richie's heart sank. The bumpy ground was
slowing him down, but the robot, on its two
massive metal legs, was just as fast as before. He
wasn't going to make it.

Then he had a piece of luck. He saw a dirt
road—probably used by engineers to service the
pylons—and swerved onto it.

The ground shook under the robot's massive
iron feet, and bounced Richie's truck. It was almost on top of him. It bent down to grab the
truck, but, Richie, watching carefully in his side
mirror, swerved at the last second. The robot's
metal grabs swished past, closing on nothing,
and Richie roared under the pylons. The robot
came after him, crashing through the power
lines, which broke and danced around, spark-
ing, hitting the metal Goliath with millions of
volts of electricity.

As Richie sped across the field, the robot, getting more and more entangled in the live wires,
vibrated and shook.

Inside it, the Martian operator was getting no
response from his controls. The robot slipped,
bringing down two of the towers, and crashed
on its back. It convulsed for a few moments,

then its lights went out. Richie U-turned toward the highway.

Las Vegas was a full-blown war zone. Jets and helicopters fought a losing battle with flying saucers in the sky, while, on the ground, Martian troops steadily pushed back the army forces.

The Treasure Island Hotel was a smoking ruin, so, too, the Dunes, the Tropicana, Circus Circus, and the Mirage.

In their relentless march up the Strip, the Martians had spared only one building: the Debbie Reynolds Hotel. Why that one? But, anyway, the front line had now reached Caesar's Palace.

On the north side of the freeway, Byron, Tom Jones, Barbara, Cindy, and Joe Weinberg were sneaking through a broken gate. They had risked death numerous times in their journey from the Luxor, and now were close to the airfield.

The whole neighborhood was thick with black, acrid smoke. You couldn't see more than ten feet in front of you. The sky was popping with tracer fire from distant army artillery, trying to shoot down the flying saucers. Barbara was suddenly filled with doubt.

"This is the wrong way!"

Byron looked around, his pharoah costume

now streaked with dirt. "It's a shortcut. The air-strip's on the other side!"

"Bullshit!" yelled Joe Weinberg. "It's over there." He pointed up the street.

"Trust me," said Byron. "I know what I'm doing. Come on!"

"Hey," sneered Joe Weinberg, "just because you're dressed like King Tut doesn't mean you're a leader!"

Byron hurried on. The others followed, entering a junkyard of old, discarded Las Vegas signs.

Keeping their heads low, and holding their ears to cut down the noise, they weaved their way through the surreal junkyard. Byron led them past a massive silver slipper and a giant bulb-encrusted Aladdin's lamp. Joe Weinberg was losing confidence in the whole expedition.

"This isn't right," he said to Barbara. "We're lost! He's led us into a maze!" Barbara looked at him anxiously.

"We're all going to get killed," yelled Joe. "I'm going back to the hotel." He turned and headed back the way they had come.

"No, wait!" shouted Barbara.

But it was too late, he was gone.

Joe grumbled to himself as he passed a giant fish and a bucking-bronco sign. "Assholes! Why

did I listen to them? I should have stayed in the hotel!'' He froze. A Martian was staring at him.

''Oh shit.''

Joe was in a kind of clearing. There was no cover close by. There was nowhere to run. He put up his hands.

''See?'' he said to the Martian. ''I surrender. Okay? You understand what that means? Surrender?''

The Martian didn't move. Joe took a tentative step toward him.

''Lookit, you're intelligent beings—let's cut a deal. I can help you! I'm a lawyer! You want to conquer the world, you're gonna need lawyers, right?''

The Martian raised his weapon.

Sweating with fear, Joe Weinberg made a last-ditch attempt to save his skin. He took off his watch and held it out. ''You know what this is?''

The Martian, curious, lowered his raygun.

''It's a watch.'' He shook the watch.

''Take it! Take it—go on! It's a Rolex!''

Kapow! The Martian reduced Joe Weinberg to a skeleton with one raygun burst. His bones clattered to the ground.

Blam! The Martian's head exploded. He fell back dead. Barbara Land was some distance away, inside the ''O'' of the Golden Nugget sign. Her raygun emitted tendrils of purple smoke.

"Good shot!" said Tom Jones, climbing up beside her.

"Pity I was too late," she said.

They were joined by Byron and Cindy. Cindy was excited.

"Look!" she pointed. "Over there! The airfield!"

In the gap between two signs, they could see a piece of the airfield, a hangar, and a burning plane.

Chapter 27

O, horrible! O, horrible! most horrible!

—William Shakespeare, *Hamlet*

Richie raced down the highway. At the next corner, he'd be able to see the retirement home.

There was no clear plan in his mind, except to get Grandma and escape. Maybe he could drive to Kentucky, keeping off the main highways? Maybe they could survive up there in the hills, where the hillbillies lived? People had been living there for centuries, avoiding the census, making their own whiskey, and paying no taxes. If the IRS couldn't find them, the Martians probably couldn't, either.

Richie came around the bend. He saw the retirement home in the distance and his face fell. Smoke and flames were belching from its roof. The Martians were there already! Damn!

Anger brewed inside Richie like a noxious gas. He glanced around the cab. Where was the gun? It had been on the passenger seat. Then he saw it, his father's army service revolver, in the foot well on the passenger side. He hadn't thought to grab the box of shells on the table, so he only had the six rounds that were in the chamber. He leaned down, picked it up, and accelerated down the slope toward Grandma, and probably his own death.

In the Nightingale Retirement Home, Martians were torturing and killing the elderly residents. Ordinarily quiet and peaceful, the place now looked like a medieval painting of Hell by Heronimous Bosch.

On the porch, an old man in a wheelchair sped by, in flames. In the lobby, an old lady with a walker, hobbled at high speed toward the entrance door. A Martian was peeking at her from around the corner of the corridor wall. Pzzzzzztt! The old lady became an instant fireball.

Down one of the hallways, three Martians pushed a large gun mounted on a trolley. This was a new, experimental weapon, which they had been assigned to test out. The gun was bulbous and futuristic-looking, with lots of curling wires sprouting out of it.

As the gun crew pushed the weapon down the hallway, a door opened and a nice old lady looked out. Behind her were three very nervous geriatrics.

"Hello!" she said.

The Martians fired their rayguns and blew them all to hell. Then they pushed the experimental weapon to the end of the corridor.

One of the Martians opened the door to Grandma's room and looked in. Grandma was sitting in her rocker, wearing headphones, listening to the music of Slim Whitman, oblivious to what was happening.

The Martian motioned to the others to be silent and come look. They all peered through the doorway, and stifled the urge to giggle. Rocking gently, eyes closed, a shawl across her lap, Grandma bore a comic resemblance to Whistler's Mother. The Martians pushed the door open and, very quietly, wheeled in the futuristic gun.

On his way into the grounds, Richie passed a flying saucer parked on the grass verge. There were no Martians around, so he assumed they were all in the home. He drove down the gravel drive. There were incinerated corpses everywhere, littering the front garden. He pulled up

outside the entrance. One end of the building was on fire.

Richie, now entirely inside the cloud of his anger, swung out of the truck, gun in hand. He stepped over the skeletons on the porch, and pushed through the entrance doorway. The lobby was a grisly sight, but he didn't stay to look. He headed for Grandma's room.

In Washington, in the War Room, the atmosphere was gloomy. Some time ago, the Pentagon had been razed to the ground, and communications between the military commanders and their troops had almost completely broken down. People were going through the motions of concocting new strategies, and, as best they could, consolidating losses, and directing retreats.

General Decker tore a sheet of paper from one of the computer printers, and crossed the floor. "Mr. President?"

"Yes, what is it?" said Dale, like a dead man.

"The computer says, if they maintain this level of assault," said the general, "they will destroy the world in six days."

The President glanced at Decker, and a strange thought struck him. "In six days God created the world," he said, "and in six days it will be destroyed."

Decker was about to say something like, "Don't you think that's a little fatalistic?" but thought better of it. He had no solutions, either.

In New York, the island of Manhattan looked like a scuttled battleship—a big, black, smoking hulk. Brooklyn was on fire, blazing out of control; Queens had been completely demolished, and the South Bronx looked pretty much like it always does. Oddly, the Statue of Liberty was unharmed. For some reason, the Martians had spared it, leaving it to reign over the smoldering boneyard that had once been the Big Apple.

In Jolly Old England, flying saucers blasted the city of London. One blew up St. Paul's Cathedral, another destroyed Buckingham Palace, a third disintegrated the Houses of Parliament and Big Ben, a fourth flew along the course of the River Thames, blowing up the bridges.

Martians were landing everywhere, and the same scenario, as everywhere else, was playing itself out: human annihilation at the hands of the invincible Martian foe.

In India, a spaceship hovered over the Taj Mahal. At a safe distance, a group of Martians prepared to take a photograph of this world-famous landmark. The spaceship fired, the Taj Mahal exploded, and the Martians got their picture!

In the South Pacific, a flying saucer swooped over Easter Island, celebrated for the giant stone heads that brood over the beaches. The natives trembled as the spaceship approached and a circular hatch opened underneath it. A burning orb emerged, held by a mechanical hand. The natives took cover.

The hand threw the flaming orb, like a bowling ball, at a row of giant heads. Craaack! The giant ball knocked them all over. Inside the cockpit, the three Martian pilots whooped with glee and slapped hands. A strike!

Back in the United States, a crowd of tourists visiting Mount Rushmore were alarmed to see a spaceship soar up to the famous carved heads of the Presidents. An intensely bright zigzagging beam pulsed from the ship and into the stone faces. Clouds of smoke and rock dust billowed from the side of the mountain. The tourists ran down to their cars in the parking lot. Petrified, tires squealing, they hightailed it out to the highway.

After a while, the spaceship stopped firing at the mountainside and the barrel retracted, to be replaced by a wide-caliber hose. A jet of liquid shot out, dispersing the smoke and washing away the dust. The Presidents' heads emerged, but now they had been recarved into the features of famous Martians!

In the retirement home, Richie, gun in hand, crept down the hallway toward Grandma's room. He could hear the crackling roar of the fire at the other end of the home, and parts of the building collapsing. Also, from somewhere far off, he heard the sound of a woman wailing. Then the wailing stopped.

Very carefully, he stepped over two hot, steaming skeletons, and tiptoed up to Grandma's door. The door was ajar. Richie couldn't believe his eyes. Three Martians were pointing a big futuristic gun directly at Grandma's head!

He charged in, firing at the Martians. Bang! Bang! Bang! Bang! One of them fired a raygun blast, which narrowly missed, singeing Richie's hair, and disintegrating the door behind him. He fell, and his gun bounced out of his hand.

Grandma turned her head sharply, pulling the headphone cord out of the socket on the record player—redirecting the music from the headphone output to the speakers. The room instantly filled with the sound of Slim Whitman yodeling.

All of a sudden, queasy expressions creased the faces of the Martians. Their eyeballs bulged, their cerebra vibrated, and small green capillaries burst in their brains!

Grandma peered at her visitors, and adjusted

her spectacles. Richie got up—he couldn't believe what he was seeing. The Martians were dancing up and down, shrieking, their brains expanding and contracting. The first Martian's brain exploded inside its dome, and he fell dead! Grandma turned to Richie, very agitated.

"Oh, Richie! I'm awful worried! Look at these men here! I think they're sick!"

The second Martian's brain exploded. Richie scratched his head.

"What's killing them?" he said.

The third Martian's brain blew up, covering the inside of his dome with gunk. He dropped, lifeless, across the futuristic gun.

"What's killing 'em?" repeated Richie.

Grandma looked at him guiltily. "I think it's my music."

Richie nodded and listened to the warbling Country notes of Slim Whitman. Then he looked at the dead Martians and knew what had to be done.

In Washington, in the War Room, General Decker heard something different—a strange scratching noise coming from outside the door.

"Everybody quiet!" he shouted. The War Room personnel continued what they were doing.

"Quiet!!" screamed Decker.

And the room fell silent.

"I can hear something."

Everyone held their breath and listened. Gradually, the pitter-patter of tiny feet became audible. People looked at one another nervously. What did this mean? Suddenly a loud explosion smashed a hole through the steel door! Everyone ducked.

A moment later, Decker raised his head. Through the smoke, he saw a small hand appear through the hole in the door and toss in a pulsating green ball. The ball hit the floor with a *clunk* and rolled to a stop in the center of the room. Expecting an explosion, Decker bobbed down. Nothing happened.

Behind his desk, at the head of the room, the suspense was killing President Dale. He took a peek, and saw, coming through the hole, the Martian leader and six Martian officers. The officers covered the room with their weapons and the Martian leader walked over to the green ball, picked it up, and, holding it level with his face, shook it. The greenness inside evaporated, revealing a model of a baby Martian, with snow falling around it. It was a Martian snow globe toy! The Martian leader quacked something to his officers, and they all laughed.

Decker was furious. This was too much! The Martians were mocking them! He drew both his

pistols and stood up. The Martians looked at him curiously. Decker glared back.

"You think you can come over here . . ." he yelled, ". . . and do whatever you want?"

Spit shot out of his mouth.

"Well, *you don't know human beings*!!"

He marched forward, firing both pistols. The Martian leader issued an order.

Dodging, bullets bouncing off their body-armor, five Martians rushed at Decker and shoved him against the wall, knocking the guns out of his hands. Decker struggled violently.

"We will never give up!" he roared.

The Martian leader took out a tiny little gun. It looked like a Cracker Jack toy. "We will fight you and fight you to the last man! We will *never surrender*!" yelled Decker, trying to shake off his assailants. To his surprise, they suddenly let go of him and stepped away. Then he saw why. The Martian leader fired! A bizarre, fluctuating light emanated from the little gun, flowed across the room, and hit Decker in the chest.

"Goddamn you to hell!" he bellowed.

Then Decker began to shrink. In less than ten seconds he was only three inches high! Some of the War Room staff watched, astonished, as Decker ran, squeaking, across the floor, shaking both his fists.

"Damn you to hell, you ugly Martian pecker-head!" he piped, in a tiny voice.

The Martian leader looked down at the teeny general and stepped on him, squashing him flat.

Terrified, some of the humans made a dash for the door. The Martians opened fire. The President ran from his desk, hoping to get behind the enemy without being noticed. If he could do that, he could sneak out through the hole in the door. But one of the Martians spotted him and leveled his raygun. Mitch, the Secret Service man, hurled himself in front of Dale and Pzzzzttt! he died—taking the blast meant for the President.

Raygun fire lacerated the War Room, destroying everything and everyone. The President ducked behind a steel chair on castors, and moved around behind it, using it as a shield. After a few minutes, the President was the only one left alive. When he realized this, a strange mood came over him. Surrounded by the bodies of his colleagues, President Dale felt oddly anointed, as if chosen by the Almighty for a sacred task. He knew his purpose: to plead the cause of the human race. He stood up, all fear gone, and walked toward the Martian leader.

"Why are you doing this?" he asked. "Isn't the Universe big enough for the both of us? What is wrong with you people?"

There was a tone of sincerity in Dale's voice that was so compelling the Martian leader raised his hand to his comrades, indicating they were not to fire.

"We could work together. Why be enemies? Just because we're different? Is that why?"

Dale had never been so presidential. All the game-playing, all the bullshit of modern politics dropped away. The human race was under threat of total annihilation. It needed a leader—a spokesman—and James Dale rose to the occasion.

"We could work together!" he said. "Think how much we could do! Think how strong we would be! Earth and Mars together! There's nothing we couldn't accomplish! Think about it! Why destroy when you can create?"

The Martian leader nodded his head. He seemed to be impressed.

"We can have it all—or we can smash it all. Which is better? Why can't we settle our differences? Why can't we work things out?" Dale looked imploringly into the Martian leader's face. "Why can't we just get along?"

There was a pregnant pause. The Martian leader lowered his head. He seemed to be thinking something over. When he looked up, Dale saw a large tear run from his eye and down his bony cheek.

The Martian leader raised his right hand and offered it to the President. A little surprised, Dale stepped forward and clasped it warmly. They shook.

Then a strange thing happened. The Martian leader's hand detached itself from his wrist and scurried up the President's arm! It had a shiny metal tail that came out of the stump of the wrist and was curled up like a scorpion's tail. The hand stopped on Dale's shoulder and uncurled its tail, waving it in the air.

"What is that?" said the President.

The hand scampered onto the top of his back. "What's going on?"

The Martians looked at him, cold and implacable. Dale tried to brush the mechanical hand-monster off him, but it ran down his spine, uncurled its tail, and jabbed it into the President's back! The spike went through his heart, and out the front of his chest.

The President looked down, horrified, then fell backward, dead, on the floor map of the world. The spike-tail extended itself, like a telescope. It had a hinged tip. The tip flipped open and the Martian flag snapped out!

The Martian leader looked at the dead President, with the Martian flag impaled in his chest, lying on the map of the world, and was satisfied.

Chapter 28

He was a man, take him for all in all,
I shall not look upon his like again.

—William Shakespeare, *Hamlet*

The dire predicament of humanity seemed to be echoed in the night sky. There was no moon and there were no stars. It was as if the Universe itself had turned its back on the human experiment. Mayhap Darwin was right? Survival of the fittest was the only law. The Martians were superior, ergo the human race was doomed to extinction. But, the many people who were thinking this way, did not know about Richie Norris and his grandma.

Richie was driving his pickup into what was left of Perkinsville. Grandma was in the passenger seat. In the back of the truck were two large speakers taken from the Nightingale Retirement

Home. Richie had lashed them with ropes to the bumper and connected them to Grandma's record player, which he'd wired to the car battery. The Slim Whitman album was blasting out at maximum volume.

They drove toward the still-burning donut shop. Lit devilishly by the flickering flame-light, three Martians were looting. Richie saw one carrying a TV. Another was carrying a big box of donuts. They noticed Richie's truck, then heard the music. Apprehension turned to fear, turned to horror in their faces. They clutched their domes.

Grandma watched them dance, squeal, and drop dead, as they drove past. Richie grinned in triumph.

"Okay! Next stop, the radio station!"

The truck disappeared into the smoke down Main Street, its speakers blaring.

In wartorn Las Vegas, at the private airfield, Byron, Tom Jones, Barbara, and Cindy entered through the back door of a dimly lit hangar. Standing before them, in the darkness, was a shiny white twin-engine Cessna.

"There it is!" said Barbara, in a sharp whisper.

Byron sized up the situation and turned to Tom Jones. "Tom, get it started up."

Then he addressed Cindy. "Cindy, help me get the doors!"

Byron and Cindy crossed to the hangar doors. Tom Jones pulled the chocks away from the wheels as Barbara unlocked the cockpit.

Thankfully, the radio station, in Topeka, was undamaged. Richie had found an engineer hiding in the basement. Now they were in Studio B, ready to put the yodeling vocals of Slim Whitman on the air.

"You be careful now," said Grandma to the engineer. "Don't scratch it." The engineer lowered the needle onto the record.

In the airplane hangar, in Las Vegas, Tom Jones jumped into the pilot's seat and started flicking switches on the instrument panel. Barbara climbed into the copilot's seat, watching him anxiously.

"Tom, are you sure you can fly this?"

"Yes, I think so," said Tom Jones, frowning with concentration. Some of the controls were a little unfamiliar, so he did a quick test of the instrumentation. One of the knobs he turned was the AM/FM radio. For a moment, the cockpit filled with Slim Whitman, singing, "I'm Casting My Lasso Towards the Sky." Barbara

raised her eyebrows. Tom Jones quickly shut it off.

"Who put *that* on?!" he expostulated.

Byron and Cindy pulled at the large hangar door. Cindy, discombobulated by the day's events, was pulling the wrong way.

"It's stuck!" she hissed.

"No, this way!" said Byron, pulling at the large handle. Cindy pulled in the same direction, and the hangar door slid open.

Looking out over the airfield, their blood froze. Less than fifty yards away were at least a hundred Martians. They were standing at attention, four rows deep. Their commanding officer, accompanied by another Martian, was inspecting them. Byron recognized the other Martian's long, iridescent cloak—it was none other than the Martian ambassador!

"They haven't seen us!" said Byron. "Quick!"

He pulled Cindy behind the door. Cindy was trying hard not to panic. Byron glanced back at the plane. The propellers were turning, the engines were warming up. Then he peered out at the Martians.

Something changed in Byron. His eyelids drooped slightly, half covering his eyeballs. It was this "sleepy" look that used to disturb his opponents in the ring. Byron's entire physical demeanor hardened. Cindy, too, noticed the

change. It was as if the human part of him had receded, leaving the animal in command.

"Cindy, you go," he murmured, in a low growl. "I'll draw them off."

"What?"

He gave Cindy the raygun he'd been carrying. "I'm staying. I'll distract them. Soon as you get a chance, take off."

"No! I'm not leaving you!"

"Just do it," said Byron, pushing her away. "Go!"

Cindy ran to the plane.

In the small cockpit, Tom and Barbara had seen the large company of Martians, and were terrified. They didn't stand a chance. They'd be blown apart before they even reached the runway. Barbara was all out of ideas. She looked at Tom's manly profile, and could tell he was all out of ideas, too. Cindy scrambled into the cockpit behind them.

"What's he doing?" asked Barbara, referring to Byron, who was still standing at the hangar door.

"He said he's going to draw them off so we can escape!"

"Oh my God!" said Tom Jones. "Look!"

Byron walked out toward the Martians.

"Oh no!" said Cindy.

"He's flipped!" said Barbara.

They all watched Byron march, head high, toward the Martian platoon.

"We can't leave him!" said Cindy, her eyes welling with tears.

"Oh, God . . ." said Barbara, and started chanting under her breath.

Outside, on the tarmac, Byron greeted the enemy. "Hi, guys how ya doin'?"

The Martians looked at him. Some of them raised their guns. Byron held out his hands.

"Look, no weapon."

The Martian ambassador regarded Byron quizzically and indicated for the troops not to fire.

They all watched him with curiosity as he jogged on his toes, away from the hangar, loosening his shoulders and blowing his breath in and out. Maybe it was his pharoah costume that made them pause, or maybe it was his bizarre behavior? Who ever knew with Martians?

Byron jogged farther away from the hangar, put up his fists and began shadowboxing. Fascinated, the Martian platoon followed him. After he'd led them a good distance, he turned to face them.

"Come on! Come on! What are you, a bunch of wussies?"

The Martian ambassador squawked some-

thing to his men, then headed toward the African-American pugilist.

The Martians relaxed and watched their chief make a few fight-moves of his own. The ambassador was clearly a bantamweight, but he was fast. Byron was a heavyweight, slow and over-the-hill.

"Okay, Mr. Ambassador . . ."

Byron bounced forward, throwing a left hook. The ambassador dodged and landed three sharp jabs into Byron's solar plexus. Byron grunted. The Martians cheered. The ambassador acknowledged the applause and danced in a circle around Byron, getting through his defenses with a slew of body blows. The ambassador didn't hit hard, but he hit a lot.

But Byron Williams, veteran of 112 boxing tournaments, knew strategy. He let the ambassador get confident. Byron needed only one punch. He waited for the right opening, studying his opponent's tactics, until he could predict where the speedy little homunculus was going to go.

The opportunity came. Byron got him with a right uppercut, cracking his dome and ripping it from his suit. Oxygen flew in, mixed with the nitrogen and exploded in clouds of green acid gas.

The Martian ambassador died, squealing and

shuddering on the ground. There was a silence. The Martian troops were shocked. Byron bounced on the balls of his feet. Beyond the phalanx of Martians, he could see the Cessna taxiing out of the hangar.

Three of the biggest Martians stepped forward and put up their fists. Byron kept them in his sights, breaking eye contact with one, only to engage with the next, as they circled around him. He sensed one coming at him from behind, spun and delivered a straight right cross. The Martian went down. He took a couple of rabbit punches in the guts, then dodged, feinted, jabbed the second Martian and smashed the third in the thorax with his world-famous left hook. He felt the ugly critter's rib cage break apart. Suddenly, there were five more Martians swatting at him. Byron threw a whirlwind of punches, left and right. Domes smashed, shoulder blades snapped, chests broke . . . All around him, furious Martians boxed and died.

Sweat poured down Byron's face as he fought Martian after Martian. Panting, breathless, his knuckles bleeding, he battled the unending sea of assailants, like a mythic hero of old. But he could not stem the tide. The odds were too great. . . .

Across the airfield, on the runway, the plane reached takeoff speed.

Byron, hit from all sides, lost his footing, and fell. Kicking and punching, the Martians swarmed over him, like vultures on a carcass.

The plane rose into the sky. Tom Jones, Barbara, and Cindy, choked with emotion, gazed down at the battling hero below.

"Oh no! No!" cried Barbara.

"Byron! Byron! Oh, God! I love him! I love him!" wailed Cindy hysterically.

In Louise's apartment in Washington, Louise felt a psychic shiver. She was barricaded in the bedroom, with her two sons.

"Something's happened," said Louise.

Cedric and Neville glanced at her. Her eyes were staring, like she'd seen a ghost.

"What's up, Ma? Are you all right?" said Cedric.

"Something's happened to Byron," said Louise, haunted.

Chapter 29

How art thou fallen from heaven,
O Lucifer, son of the morning!

—Isaiah 14:12

Ae fond kiss, and then we sever;
Ae fareweel, and then for ever!

—Robert Burns

For the past twenty-four hours, Richie had been broadcasting the message—and he was still going strong. Grandma kept refilling his coffee mug, while the engineer continued to find more wave bands on which to spread the country music of deliverance to the world.

In the suburbs of Baltimore, in a heavily fortified kitchen, a woman turned on her radio. The yodeling arpeggios of Slim Whitman flowed into the room, and she heard the voice of Richie Norris explaining what the music could do.

In the South of France, in the catacombs of a monastery, nine miles north of Aix, a group of monks listened to Whitman's country verses and recorded them on their old Grundig tape recorder, for use against the Martian enemy.

Outside Las Vegas, three armored cars, with huge speakers mounted above the wheel guards, moved down the damaged highway, broadcasting the music. A flying saucer, passing overhead, began to wobble. The wobbling intensified until the whole spaceship shook. Inside, its evil invader occupants were dropping dead. Rudderless, with no one at the helm, the flying saucer spun earthward and crashed into the Hotel Excalibur.

In London, England, a naval helicopter, with specially mounted speakers, flew over the ruins of Westminster Bridge, broadcasting the music. A regiment of Martians, marching along the Thames River embankment, danced, squealed, and expired.

A squadron of helicopters flew above the ruined city of Washington, blaring out the melodies. In the sky, spaceships quivered, collided, and crashed while, on the ground, Martians contorted and shook, their brains bursting inside their domes.

On the South Side, opposite Martin Luther King High, Cedric and Neville ran, pushing a shopping cart containing a ghetto blaster—pumping out Slim Whitman at full volume. Fleeing from them were four Martians—their heads exploding!

Along the Atlantic Coast, just north of Savannah, Georgia, the Martian flagship was pursued by a Phantom jet with speakers mounted under its wings. Inside the spaceship, in the command chamber, the Martian leader clung to his throne, his entire body vibrating. His lieutenants convulsed on the floor, screeching. Suddenly, the floor tilted at forty-five degrees.

In the Specimen Chamber, the Martians in white coats slid down the angled floor, screaming in their death agonies. Their biological samples tumbled off the shelves. Donald Kessler's organs and body parts were yanked from their life-support tubes, and his head bounced onto the floor.

Nathalie dropped from above, landing hard. Her head separated from its chihuahua body, and slithered into the head of Donald Kessler. Donald could feel himself losing consciousness, but the abrupt collision with Nathalie's face made him open his eyes.

"Good-bye, darling, I wish things could have been different!" he croaked.

"So do I!" gasped Nathalie, tears in her eyes. "Good-bye. I love you . . ." Donald's vision was breaking up. He could sense the nearness of the void.

"I love you, too, Nathalie," he wheezed.

With her last breath, Nathalie kissed him on the lips.

The Martian flagship crashed into the ocean, foamed for a moment on the surface, then sank into the deep.

A surviving horde of a mere forty-four flying saucers fled the Planet Earth, some of them colliding in their desperate hurry to escape. Humiliated, these pitiful remnants of the once-grand Martian fleet bolted, shamefully, back to Mars.

Near the Tahoe Caves, the sun peeped over the mountains. It was dawn. A robin, on a branch, fluffed out its feathers and began to sing. The air was crisp and fresh.

Emerging from the mouth of a cave came Barbara, Cindy, and Tom Jones. Rubbing their eyes, they made their way to a rocky shelf, which overlooked the spectacular river basin below. No one wanted to speak. They stood, absorbing

nourishment from Nature, and were shyly joined by a flock of mountain goats. It was a new day.

In Washington, D.C., people were cleaning up. By the fallen Washington Monument, and along Constitution Avenue, people filled wheelbarrows with Martian corpses. Throughout the streets, people worked together, searching for survivors amid the ruins and stacking debris in neat piles. On Pennsylvania Avenue, a large bonfire of dead Martians was blazing. The whole city was alive with men, women, and children cleaning up the mess. No one spoke. The silence was so intense you could hear it.

Chapter 30

Rebellion to tyrants is obedience to God.

—John Bradshaw

A day of heaping rubble, sweeping, scrubbing and generally cleaning house, left the populous tired and happy. Grief at the millions of tragedies—all the loved ones lost—had not yet kicked in. People were high on their own survival. There was a total openness among people; no one spoke a lie, no one felt or acted superior, everyone was immersed in the same loving mood of equality.

At the end of the day, as the sun set, a small crowd gathered on the steps of the ruined Capitol. Many had come, attracted by the halogen glare of the TV lights. A student TV crew was filming an award ceremony.

Six Marines, in crumpled uniforms, stood

halfway up the steps, next to a Mariachi band, some of whom were bandaged, others on crutches.

A few steps below them, holding two medals, was Taffy, flanked by an elderly mailman and a priest. In front of her sat Grandma Norris in her wheelchair. Next to Grandma stood Richie. They had both been flown to Washington, from Kansas, in an army transport plane.

The crowd watched as Taffy held up a medal. "Florence Norris," she said, in the loudest voice she could muster, "I am proud to present you with the Congressional Medal of Honor. The highest decoration our nation can bestow." She leaned down and hung the medal around Grandma's neck. Then she kissed her on both cheeks.

"Thank you, dear," said Grandma, her eyes shining. But she raised a finger and gave a warning look. "Please don't let this happen again!"

Taffy nodded, not sure how to react, and turned to Richie.

Pascal said that love is not love if it doesn't happen at first sight. Richie looked at Taffy and saw she was beautiful. Taffy looked at Richie and felt the color come into her face. She forced herself to concentrate on the job at hand. "Richard Norris," she cried, loud enough for the crowd to hear, "on behalf of my parents, who

could not be here today, for saving the world from the Martians, I hereby award you the Medal of Honor."

Richie lowered his head. She put the medal around his neck. He looked up. Their eyes met. Suddenly she felt very shy.

"You don't have to kiss me if you don't want," he said.

"I've got to," said Taffy. "It's part of the ceremony." She kissed him quickly on both cheeks.

"I, uh, prepared a speech. Is that okay?" asked Richie.

Taffy was trying to act professional. "Yes," she said, "I think that's very appropriate."

"Okay, uh . . ." Richie took out a crumpled piece of paper and, hesitantly, addressed the crowd. "Well, folks, I just want to say thank you to my grandma here, for helping to save the world. And to say that there's lots of people who did as much, and more, than I have—and they should be here now, too, getting a medal also."

At the back of the crowd, behind the Dalai Lama, stood Louise and her two sons, Cedric and Neville. Their faces were grim. They were thinking of Byron.

"So," continued Richie, "we made it. But we almost didn't. It was close. And"—he glanced at his speech—"now we must rebuild."

"Speak up! We can't hear you!" yelled some-one from the crowd.

"We must rebuild," said Richie, louder now. "We must rebuild our cities. But, maybe not the way they were before. Maybe instead of houses, we should live in teepees—it's better in a lot of ways."

Taffy felt a thrill in her heart. That's what she thought, too!

"And the environment—let's take care of it this time. And let's have a decent justice system that is based on fairness. Then we won't need so many lawyers. And psychiatrists—did they ever really help anybody? If we can get society right this time, maybe we won't need 'em!"

The crowd applauded. Richie pushed his hair away from his face and smiled. He'd just thought of something else. "And there's no need to cut military or government spending now, because that's been taken care of!"

The crowd cheered!

"The future's gonna be great! Let's go for it! I guess that's all I have to say. Thank you!"

The crowd roared. Richie glanced at Taffy.

"Was that all right?"

"Yeah."

They waited for the applause to die down, then Taffy turned to the crowd. "That's it.

Thank you for coming! Good luck! Let's get society right this time!"

The crowd cheered, then began to disperse as the Mariachi band played a rhythmic Mexican version of "The Star-Spangled Banner."

Richie and Taffy manhandled Grandma's wheelchair down the steps.

"So, what are you doing now?" asked Taffy.

"I don't know," said Richie.

"Do you have a girlfriend?"

"Uh, well, no I don't," said Richie.

They made their way down the steps to the street.

The sun had set and the night sky was filled with thousands of twinkling stars. Various sections of Washington were still burning, putting out red glares over parts of the city. But firefighters were getting organized and restoring water supplies. By the end of the night, the fires would all be out.

Acknowledgments

I'd like to thank Tim Burton, the creative force behind the whole enterprise; Larry Franco, the extraordinary producer of the film; all the people at Warner Bros., especially Bob Daly and Terry Semel, who made it happen; Scott Alexander, Colleen Atwood, Sue Berger, Danny Elfman, Jeff Field, Jill Jacobs, Alec Kamp, Larry Karaszewski, Chris Lebenzon, Tom Mack, Jack Nicholson, Eva Quiroz, Apryl Runnells, Michelle Skoby, Lisa-Marie Smith, Peter Suschitzky and Wynn Thomas.